Vin Shanley was a headteacher for a number of years, before taking early retirement in 1995. Since then he has divided his time between Billingham and Barcelona. He has recently published a book on assemblies for secondary schools and his ambition is to see Middlesborough champions of the Premier League.

John Golds has taught in London, Greece, Yorkshire and Durham. He lives in North Yorkshire and relaxes by playing squash, going to the gym and reading anything he can lay his hands on. His ambition is to see West Ham champions of the Premier League.

Classroom Clangers

Vincent Shanley
and
John Golds

ARROW

Published in the United Kingdom in 1996 by
Arrow Books

3 5 7 9 10 8 6 4

Copyright © Vincent Shanley and John Golds, 1996

The right of Vincent Shanley and John Golds to be identified as the
authors of this work has been asserted by them in accordance with
the Copyright, Designs and Patents Act, 1988

First published in the United Kingdom in 1996 by Arrow Books

Arrow Books Limited
Random House UK Limited
20 Vauxhall Bridge Road, London SW1V 2SA

Random House Australia (Pty) Limited
16 Dalmore Drive, Scoresby,
Victoria 3179

Random House New Zealand Limited
18 Poland Road, Glenfield,
Auckland 10, New Zealand

Random House South Africa (Pty) Limited
Box 2263, Rosebank 2121, South Africa

Random House UK Limited Reg. No. 954009

A CIP record for this book is available from the British Library

Papers used by Random House UK Limited are natural,
recyclable products made from wood grown in sustainable forests.
The manufacturing processes conform to the environmental
regulations of the country of origin.

ISBN 0 09 9970451 X

Typeset by Palimpsest Book Production Limited,
Polmont, Stirlingshire
Printed and bound in the United Kingdom

This book is dedicated to all of those who work in
the demanding field of education,
in whatever capacity.
Well done!

Contents

Introduction

Education is one aspect of life which we all share, and consequently it provides a common interest. Memories of our own education and school life frequently impinge on our psyche, especially if we have children undergoing the process. While education is a very serious subject, it does have a lighter side, which in these days of cut-backs, inspections and media-concentration, is much welcome. This book is a collection of mad misprints, daft headlines and humorous anecdotes relating to the world of education. More often than not it is the unintentional jokes which are often the funniest, and this compilation contains the most amusing and comical.

1

Examinations

Examinations: those necessary evils of school life which are the source of anguish for so many pupils, and without which teachers could not motivate, have provided many mirthful moments. Strangely the *1066 and All That* rubric:

> **'Make sure you write on at least one side of the paper.'**

rarely, if ever, prompts more than quizzical and curious stares.

Examination marking in each school will bring with it a rash of collectable titbits peculiar to each institution. The following is a representative sample:

> *Question:* What was Hitler's Christian name?
> *Answer:* Heil.
> *Question:* What is a turbine?
> *Answer:* Something an Arab wears on his head.
> *Question:* What is Britain's highest award for valour in war?
> *Answer:* Nelson's Column.

Question: Who was it that didn't like the return of the Prodigal Son?

Answer: The fatted calf.

Question: What's a Hindu?

Answer: It lays eggs.

Question: Use the word 'judicious' in a sentence.

Answer: Hands that judicious can be soft as your face, with mild green Fairy Liquid.

Question: Name the four seasons.

Answer: Salt, mustard, pepper, vinegar.

Question: What changes happen to your body as you age?

Answer: When you get old, so do your bowels and you get inter-continental.

Question: What guarantees may mortgage companies insist on?

Answer: They'll insist you're well-endowed if you're buying a house.

Question: What is a co-operative?

Answer: It's a kind of shop that's not as dear as places like Marks and Spencer.

Question: How important are elections to a democratic society?

Answer: Sex can only happen when a male gets an election.

Question: What is the first thing you would do to someone who has been involved in a car accident and is immobile?

Answer: Rape them in a blanket and then give them a sweet cup of tea.

Question: What is artificial respiration commonly known as?

Answer: The kiss of death.

Question: What must you take particular care in when applying by letter for a job?

Answer: You must spell all the words write.

Question: What are steroids?

Answer: Things for keeping the carpet on the stairs.

Question: What is a common treatment for a badly bleeding nose?

Answer: Circumcision.

Question: What is the correct word to describe your father's father?

Answer: Frederick.

Question: What is the capital of Italy?

Answer: 'I'.

Question: Use 'unaware' in a sentence to show you understand its meaning.

Answer: 'Unaware' means your vest and pants.

Question: What was myxomatosis?

Answer: It was when they wiped out rabbis.

'Magellan circumcised the World with a 100-foot Clipper.'

'Red, pink, orange and flamingo are the colours of the rectum.'

'I've said goodbye to my boyhood, now I'm looking forward to my adultery.'

'Monotony means being married to the same person for all of your life.'

'When my goldfish died, I was really gutted.'

'In the Junior School we used to do PE with apparatus in our knickers.'

'A lot of companies have been considering the use of random urine tests to flush out employees who take drugs.'

'I always know when it is time to get up
when I hear my mother sharpening the
toast.'

One can go so far as to say that religion is not
sacrosanct, as can be seen from these 'clangers' from
The Southern Examining Board:

'Jesus was born by supernatural contraception.'
'The tenth leopard when he saw he had
lost his spots went back to say "thank
you".'

'Jesus healed people with very bad illnesses;
like the widow of Nairn's son; he was so ill he
was dead.'
'The bishop wears a martyr on his head.'
'Christians go on pilgrimage to Lords.'
'The foreskin is cut by a molar.'
'The first book of the Bible is called Genius.'
'One commandment is not to omit adultery.'

Question: **Who is the Devil?**
Answer: **I don't believe in the Devil. It's like Santa
Claus – it's your Dad all the time!**

Definitions of words often reveal that a pupil may
have difficulties in spelling – or is it hearing? – or
simply understanding . . . ?

BENIGN . . . What you be after you be eight
CAESAREAN SECTION . . . A district in Rome
**COMA . . . A punctuation mark – a bit like
a full stop**
ENEMA . . . Someone who is not your friend
FIBULA . . . A small lie
MORBID . . . When there is a bigger offer
**NODE . . . When you have known somebody for a
long time**
SEIZURE . . . Roman Emperor
**TERMINAL ILLNESS . . . When you are sick at
the airport**

TIBIA . . . A country in North Africa
VARICOSE . . . Nearby
VEIN . . . Conceited

An abundance of common sense and calmness is embodied in the answer given by a Middlesbrough Junior School girl to a question contained in the 1995 Science Key Stage 2 SATs exam:

> *Question:* **How would you separate a solution of salt and water?**
> *Answer:* **Well, first of all, I'd sit down and have a nice cup of tea.**

According to an advertisement in the *Wirral Globe*, success in exams is extremely easy:

> '**Exams. Learn the principles of success in studying and passing exams. One day course.**'

Pupils should not underestimate their own abilities. The *Associated Examining Board* reports:

> '**The Board's advisers do not feel that critical appreciation difficult for 16-year-olds, but they consider it is entirely appropriate, in terms of an O-level examination in Drama, to expect candidates both to evaluate their own work and to write critical appraisals of plays and performances seen. Criticisms can be at various levels, and candidates who write at the level of, say, the *Sunday Times* Drama Critic would receive full marks.**'

The GCSE boards are always stringent in applying their rules and their verdicts are pretty final. There are no grounds for misinterpreting this directive, as reported in the *Times Educational Supplement* (TES):

> **'GCSE candidates: No refunds will be made except on compassionate grounds (e.g. death of candidate).'**

It does come as a welcome relief to know that there are sections of the profession who can spot where the real priorities lie, and express genuine concern and sympathy:

> **'Teachers in Liverpool have noticed that pupils are depressed after the City's soccer teams have lost a match. Now a team of psychologists from Liverpool University is going to question 200 boys in eight secondary schools. A research psychologist, Mr Kevin Fleisch, who is running the survey, said yesterday: "It is worrying to think what happens at Easter-time, when CSE examinations are going on at the same time as critical League and Cup matches."'**
>
> **(*Guardian*)**

But back to the 'clangers' – this time from a school in Whitley Bay and the Year 9 History Exam:

> **'. . . the queen was Marryanne Twanet'**
> **'. . . bias mean overagjagderating.'**
> **'The Second Estate was the nobles . . . These were the type of people you would have to put your coat over a muddy pool for.'**
> **'Mozart was a child orgy.'**

From time to time the questions set seem unreasonable, especially when those setting the papers, it is suspected, would have no small problem answering themselves. Such a question appeared in the SEG Sociology GCSE 1990 Paper 2 exam:

> **'Question 5 (e): How might the National Curriculum improve the education system in the United Kingdom?' (8 marks)**

Perhaps whoever formulated the syllabus for the entrance exam at Bradford Girls' Grammar felt that straightforward literary skills were too easy:

> **'The ability to spell, punctuate and write incoherent sentences will be tested by a piece of extended writing such as a story.'**

Sometimes questions receive realistic, if pithy, answers. A Child Care examination carried this question:

> **What are the advantages of mothers' milk over other forms of milk?**
> **Answers:**
> > **1. It's cleaner**
> > **2. It's cheaper**
> > **3. The cat can't get at it!**

It is surprising to what lengths individuals will go to pass an examination. The *Yorkshire Post* reported this item:

> **'Jordanian police have caught two teenage girls who impersonated their brothers to sit high school examinations.'**

From California, the *Los Angeles Times* reports:

'Morgan Lamb's lawyer's wife took Mr Lamb's
California state bar exams on his behalf. She
achieved the third highest score out of 7,000
applicants, after he had previously failed dismally.

Mrs Morgan Lamb dressed up as Mr Morgan
Lamb. But there was a problem: exam officials
said they 'became suspicious' because the alleged
Mr Lamb was visibly pregnant at the time. The
prosecutor claimed this week the case was one of
"yuppy greed ran amok".'

With the advent of league tables particularly, schools
will do everything they can to assist their pupils to
be successful – or will they? This notice appeared in
a North-East school:

**QUIET, PLEASE
EXAM IN PROGRESS
DO NOT PASS**

2

Headteachers
and Teachers

Headteachers are powerful individuals within their own domains, and some exhibit a pomposity and high-handedness which makes it all the more delightful when they are deflated.

> At a staff meeting in a school in Kent, the Head was still droning on 30 minutes after the 5 o'clock deadline. He eventually consulted his time-piece and exclaimed:
> 'Goodness gracious, my watch seems to have stopped.'
> Whereupon an obviously unambitious teacher retorted:
> 'Never mind your watch – use the calendar on the wall behind you!'

Other Heads can demonstrate a startling aloofness from their true purpose, as can be seen from this quote in *The Times*:

> 'Fortunately mine is an independent school, and I

am not obliged to make obeisance to the sacred
cow called education.'

Could this have been the same bumptious Head
who . . .

... when his wife settled down in bed and
remarked: 'God, your feet are cold!' he replied:
'How many times do I have to tell you – when
we're in bed, you can call me "George"!'

Headteachers can generate much animosity among
parents and staff.

When a Head from Saffron Walden had replaced
the telephone after what had clearly been a heated
discussion with a parent, the Deputy Headteacher
asked what the parent had said:
'In a nutshell, he suggested that I should follow
the advice given in Genesis 1:28 – "Go forth and
multiply!"'

From time to time, it would seem that the pressures
of the job cause some to take action in ways which
indicate quite clearly they are well on their way to the
funny-farm, if not heading for a custodial sentence.
This Head, in a report carried in the *News Chronicle*,
certainly took positive action:

'A Headmistress wrote to the North-Eastern
District Committee yesterday, saying she made
girls scrub their tongues because, "She had never
heard such an epidemic of bad language."
In a report to the Committee, it was alleged
that carbolic soap was used, and one father

complained that his daughter's mouth was so sore that she could not eat.

The Committee left the matter with the School Managers.'

The hazards of travel to and from school take on a new meaning when this report from the *Daily Herald* is considered:

'A Headmaster warned of the dangers of forcing 15-year-old boys and girls to sit three to a seat on school buses. "Are we morally justified in exposing young people, bored by twisting roads, to dangers of this sort?" he asked. Mr John Jameson, Headmaster of a Whitby, Yorkshire, School, was speaking at a public inquiry into proposed rail cuts in the town.'

The temptations of the flesh afflicting youngsters as they gyrate in various directions on a charabanc while crossing the North York Moors, pale into insignificance in the face of the multitude of very real dangers which face pupils nowadays out of school. Quite rightly, there are now in place stringent regulations pertaining to safety. Long gone are the days revealed in this snippet from the *TES*:

> **'Sometimes when I and my fellow aging Heads and ex-Heads fall a-reminiscing about the golden days of the Initial Teaching Alphabet and Ministers of Education who kept themselves decently aloof from the curriculum, we tell each other horror stories about what were once acceptable school outing practices.**
>
> **"We used to go to the Royal Show," said one veteran at such a gathering. "We'd let the kids off the coach at 10 and tell them to be back in time to go home. During the day we might see the odd one going past hanging on to the back of a tractor."'**

Another friend usually recounts, at this point, his story of how his Head took all the staff to a café in New Brighton, leaving 200 pupils building sand castles, with strict instructions not to leave the beach.

> **'When we got back the tide was coming in, and there was this long line of children with their backs to the sea-wall. The big kids were holding the little ones' heads above the water.'**

Not what would be expected of Headteachers, but it is the unexpected which catches the eye – especially when it makes the headlines as in the following case from the *Daily Mail*:

**HEADMISTRESS
SCRUBBED
TO GET PLAYGROUND**

This report from the *Daily Express* has shades of St
Trinian's about it:

> 'When the field went away, nuns tucked up their
> skirts and scampered after hounds, horses –
> and the fox. And last night at the Sacred Heart
> Convent in Woldingham, Surrey, the Headmistress,
> Mother Shanley, said delightedly: "It was a
> delightful day. We actually made a kill in the
> Convent grounds."'

Dangerous animals of the canine and child variety
appear to be threatening one area of America, according to this report from the *Los Angeles South-West
News Press*:

> 'Word was received last week that Mrs Gertrude
> Higgins, teacher of the 36th Street School, was
> severely bitten by a dog on the school grounds.
> Principal Gail Mahoney observed that it could just
> as easily have been a child.'

In attempts to stimulate great enthusiasm in spiritual
matters some Heads seem prepared to encourage and
develop numerous initiatives. The *Daily Telegraph*
records:

> 'With the approval of the Headmaster, Mr C.
> S. Walton, boys of University College School,
> Hampstead, started "Hymn Pools" on the lines
> of a football pool. Winners had to forecast hymns
> that would be chosen for morning prayers on ten
> successive mornings.'

In a school in Belfast the Headteacher, in a desperate

effort to enliven his Monday morning assembly and gain pupils' attention, began:

> '**I spent the best years of my life in the arms of another woman – my mother's!'**

Headteachers are often called upon to make speeches, and many try with varying degrees of success to make an immediate impact. The following selection has been collected over the years, and rarely has any one of them had the desired effect:

> '**Ladies and Gentlemen . . .**
>   **. . . If I haven't struck oil in 5 minutes, I'll stop boring!**
>   **. . . As good King Henry said to all of his many wives – I won't keep you long, my dears.**
>   **. . . I will know when I've said enough when you stop looking at your watches and begin shaking them.**
>   **. . . I enjoy talking to people who are intelligent, caring and sensitive, and I don't really mind talking to a group like yourselves.'**

A Headteacher from a school in Billingham tells the story of the occasion when he was making his end-of-year speech to the staff. As he fumbled for his reading spectacles to look at a few scribbled notes, he began by saying:

> '**This year has really aged me, and when you get older, you find that you gradually lose three things – your hair, your eyesight, and your . . . eh . . . eh . . .**" Before he could deliver the punch-line, which

was: " . . . I can't remember what the third is
. . . !" a quick-witted member of staff shouted out:
"Your temper!"'

The story is told of the Belfast Headteacher who
was asked to make a speech at short notice to
the PTA of his school. He had just given the 6th
Form a talk on 'Sex – A Gift from God', and so
he decided to repeat it to the parents. It went
down very well, and when he returned home, his
wife asked him what subject he had chosen to
speak on. Feeling slightly embarrassed, he decided
to tell her that his speech had been on 'Sailing
– Dinghies and Yachts'. The following week she
attended the annual school dance, and while her
husband was buying the drinks, some members
of the PTA came to have a chat with her. In the
course of conversation, they complimented her
husband on the excellent speech he had made the
previous week.

'You amaze me!' said the Head's wife, 'He
knows so very little about it. The first time he
tried it, his little red hat blew off, and the second
time, he was violently sick over the side.'

Certainly these children from a school in Wales, as
reported in the *Sunday Times*, will know a little less
about 'sex' than they might have done:

'Four pages have been cut out of all copies of a
Biology textbook used by a class of 11 to 12-year-
olds in a Cardiff Secondary School. The pages deal
with human reproduction. The Headmaster of Tŷ
Celyn Secondary, Mr A. S. J. Heale, said: "I don't
want to discuss it. It is an internal matter."'

Still on the same subject, there are occasions when Heads would wish they had not said that – or could have said that again. From a school in Ipswich it is recounted that a Head prayed thus:

> **'Bless us in our intercourse, be it for business or pleasure.'**

Another from Brighton announced:

> **'Remember it is only when you have passed all of your exams that you can be certified.'**

Others, of course, are blissfully unaware of the sacrileges they commit:

> **Jim Laker, 19-wicket hero of England's Test victory over Australia at Old Trafford in 1956, used to tell the story of how he was once invited by a school sports master to present the end-of-term prizes. The Headteacher, who knew next to nothing about cricket, introduced him like this: 'We are delighted to have with us Mr Baker, who has got 19 tickets for the Old Trafford Test.'**

Headteachers are often called upon to make presentations to colleagues who are retiring. One, in the Durham area, always has a concocted story of the poor circumstances which the unfortunate recipient had to suffer as a child. Here is a selection:

> **'X was very poor as a child – so poor in fact that she had no clothes and couldn't go out of the house. When she was four, her father went to a**

jumble sale and bought her a cap so she could look out of the window.'

'The only clothes his parents could afford were those they bought from the Army and Navy Stores. They were wonderful quality but he found it a hell of an embarrassment going to school dressed as a Japanese Admiral.'

'The family was so poor that one day he had to go to school dressed in one of his sister's frocks. What made it more embarrassing was that the teacher had an identical dress – and he was the PE master!'

'She came from a very large family, and it was not till she was sixteen years of age that she found out there were other parts of a chicken besides gravy.'

'He was so poor as a child that one day his mother gave him a button and said: "Nip next door and ask Mrs Boland if she'll put a shirt on that for you."'

'As a newly qualified teacher, he was so poorly

paid that he could not afford to buy his little lad a yo-yo for Christmas. He only managed to get him a yo.'

'He did come from a poor family, but his father was determined to give him all the opportunities he never had. He sent him to a girls' school.'

Despite all his efforts to be entertaining, at least one member of staff at a school in Woking was dissatisfied with the Head's efforts. After a rambling speech the teacher said in a stage whisper:

'He could have written that speech in his sleep. We certainly listened to it in ours.'

In Dublin the story is told of a Pope who died and went up to heaven.

He was met by St Peter and escorted to a pleasant little flat on the eighth floor. He went to bed and was awoken the next morning by bands, shouting and great excitement from the thoroughfare below. He looked out of the window and great crowds lining the road were giving a ticker-tape welcome to someone standing in a convertible in a cavalcade of tooting cars. He sought out St Peter.

'Hey!' he said. 'This is a bit rich – I arrive and nobody but you greets me. I'm quietly escorted into a small flat while this bloke – whoever he is – is given this fantastic welcome. Shouldn't I as Pope have received this type of welcome?'

'Well, you see,' said St Peter, 'We have plenty of popes here, but that man was the first headteacher to gain entry!'

Headteachers are rarely popular figures – and quite rightly – they get paid too much, and it is said that one cannot be a 'Boss' without 'ruffling feathers'.

> One Headteacher in Colchester said that in his eighteen years of headship he had only received one compliment from a member of staff, and that was somewhat backhanded:
> 'You're a b - - - - d!' he said. 'But I'll give you this – you're a fair one!'
> 'What do you mean?' asked the Head.
> 'You're a b - - - - d with everyone!'

> The apocryphal story is told of a technology teacher, in the days when they were called 'woodwork masters', who once cut the two fingers of his right hand off on the band-saw, but did not realize he had done so until he waved goodnight to the Headteacher.

Nowadays, Heads cannot even assume the full support of the governing body:

> A Headteacher from Taunton, recovering in hospital from a serious operation, was visited by the Chair of Governors, who informed him of what had transpired at the recent termly meeting. '. . . and also, you'll be delighted to hear, the governing body passed a motion to transmit to you their best wishes and a speedy recovery. It was passed by 7 votes to 6, with 5 abstentions.'

But sometimes the 'boot' (or should it be the 'glove'?) is on the other foot:

> A more robust Headteacher, prior to his

retirement, was approached by the Secretary to the Governing Body, who informed him: 'I have been asked to enquire as to what you would like as a leaving present from the Governing Body.'

Years of pent-up malice was revealed in the reply: 'Five rounds with the Chair of Governors!'

Another tale from Leeds ...

A Head was at his Catholic School one Saturday morning, catching up with the post, when he came upon two villains trying to hi-jack the Music Centre's stereo unit.

'Young man,' he said, 'Jesus and I are watching you!'

'Well, you know what Jesus and you can do!' replied the adolescent burglar.

The Head calmly turned around to where a 12-stone Rottweiler was sitting, and said:

'Jesus – take their legs off!'

Headteachers, because they are obliged frequently to

perform in public, are more liable to make gaffs and utter absurdities, which are long-remembered.

In Selby some years ago, one Headteacher said to the assembled school at the start of a new term:

> **'The Road Safety Club meets in Room 10 at 12.30 today. Are there any surviving members from last year?'**

At another assembly in Hull, a Headteacher demanded:

> **'Take care to leave the toilets clean, all of you. The Governors are in school today, and you know the first place they visit!'**

In the face of all of this incompetence, political parties of all persuasions have decided that Headteachers need training in basic management skills. Too late, alas, for one Deputy Head at a North Yorkshire comprehensive, who aspired to the reins of power.

> **He had served his school and his Headteacher loyally for 15 years, during which time the Head had never been absent – not even for a 20-minute dental check-up. During all of this time, the Head had refused to delegate anything at all.**
>
> **Then the Deputy Head's big chance came. The Head had to go to a funeral in the North of Scotland, and would be away for at least three days.**
>
> **Off he went one March morning, and his Deputy revelled in his new-found power. The Secretary made him tea; the cook showed him the menus for the week; a parent complained about the absence of homework; staff pretended to be nice**

to him. The morning went so well that he was
even looking forward to the afternoon – when a
fax arrived from Aberdeen, containing the following
message:

   'It is raining heavily here, and forecasters say the
rain is moving south. Cancel games this afternoon.'
Games, as instructed, were cancelled.

   Sad to say, the Deputy took early retirement
soon afterwards.

If insanity creeps up on some megalomaniac Heads,
other teachers have a tendency to take the law into
their hands with disastrous results. Bristol's local
paper carried a story of a teacher from a school in
Bath, who clearly demanded high standards. Failure
to comply resulted in dire consequences:

> 'A teacher slashed a 12-year-old boy's wrist with a
> knife after spotting him talking during a lesson, a
> court was told yesterday.
>
>   David Ellis told the class that he had not
> killed a pupil that day, and cut the boy's wrists
> with a craft knife, inflicting a wound that needed
> two stitches.
>
>   Ellis, 37, of Greenditch, Chilcompton, Somerset,
> who denied causing actual bodily harm, was fined
> £250 by Bath magistrates, and ordered to pay £50
> compensation and £150 costs.
>
>   He said the incident, at Beechen Cliff School in
> Bath, was a prank that went wrong.'

Two stitches is bad enough, but this teacher, as
reported in the *Times of India*, must have really
been annoyed:

> '**Enraged by the failure of his pupils to understand his teachings, Mr Dugam Jirri, a professor of mathematics from Djakarta, beat two of them unconscious and injured 13 others.**'

Clearly, detention had not been successful!

The *Guardian* reported a case which appears to throw some doubt on the Christian message of peace and forgiveness:

> '**The parents of David Bilborough, aged 14, who alleged his collar-bone was broken by a teacher during a lesson in religious instruction, say they will take legal action unless they receive a full explanation from the school.**'

But was the religious teacher a believer with a truly spiritual outlook? Well, perhaps not, if one can believe these statistics printed in *The Times*:

> '**Of 134 entrants to a Church Training College for teachers, 35 were unaware of the significance of Whit Sunday (and 19 of these were confirmed members of the Church of England); 23 were unaware that Jesus was born in Bethlehem; and 12 that Good Friday was a commemoration of His Crucifixion.**'

It is just likely this teacher belonged to the organization represented by the member of the profession described in the *Hitchin Express*:

> **The new leader of Herts teachers is a woman who left school at 15, and is now a leading figure in schoolboys' wrestling.**'

According to some individuals, if you stay in the teaching profession long enough, you can expect it to have a profound effect upon your mental condition. A report in the *Evening Standard* seems to bear this out:

> 'The prosecution said that Miss - - - - - handed two £1 notes to Mr Ronald Canning, the examiner, when he entered her car before the driving test . . . In Miss - - - - -'s defence, Mr E. Allard said she had been looking after delinquent girls for 37 years.'

But it is not always the experience of 'delinquent girls' which can take its toll. Sometimes when insanity strikes, as in the case of this individual reported in the *Luton Evening Post*, no explanation is forthcoming:

> 'When Mike Hedley, a history teacher, was given a hot cross bun, he nailed it to a beam and put his name beside it instead of eating it.'

Was he, perhaps, providing for his retirement? Or was it that everything was getting too much for him?

> Popular legend has it that an Aberdeen teacher, suffering from stress, went to see his doctor, who gave him a thorough examination. He said to him: 'I can't find anything wrong with you – it must be the drink!' Whereupon the teacher responded: 'No problem – I'll come back when you're sober.'

It is good to see that a sense of humour remains even when the diagnosis is far more serious than stress:

> A teacher from Kidderminster suffered a mild
> heart attack, and was taken to hospital, where he
> received a visit from his concerned Headteacher.
> 'Are you comfortable?' asked the Head. 'Well,'
> replied the teacher, 'I've got my own house, own
> a three-year-old Cavalier, and get away for three
> weeks' holiday a year. Does that answer your
> question?'

How ignorant can you get? Well, quite a bit more
if you are both a teacher and an aspiring politician.
The *Dyfed County Echo* reports on what happens when
these two professions merge:

> 'Oslo is the capital of Norway, and is not in
> Sweden, as we incorrectly stated last week in a
> report of a meeting of Presli District Council. The
> insertion of "Sweden" into a report of remarks by
> former geography teacher, Cllr W. Lloyd Evans,
> was intended by the editor to give greater clarity.'

Being a Headteacher is stressful in the extreme,
especially with all the paperwork involved. One way
to ease the pain is to cultivate a hobby – or at least
an allotment. What a shame, then, when red tape
prevents even this innocent pleasure.

> Such was the sad case of Headteacher Ian Gray.
> The Department of the Environment banned him
> from cultivating parsnips on his allotment on the
> grounds that their roots might damage ancient
> remains that were thought to be there. He was
> also required to remove the existing vegetables
> and then complete a separate form for each

parsnip, assuring the department that the historical
artefacts were no longer under any threat from his
root crops.

A teacher and a preacher were obviously trying to
highlight the central Christian message as reported in
the *Portsmouth News*, and must certainly have made
an impact:

> 'Assembly at the City of Portsmouth Girls' School
> began as a religious teacher, Mr R. Milliken,
> crossed the stage of the hall on a skateboard,
> colliding with the Minister of Paulsgrove Baptist
> Church (the Revd K. W. Rayson). It was a
> pre-arranged encounter to begin dialogue about
> building life on Christian foundations.'

It is not all ministers who would be prepared to be
so co-operative and suffer a loss of dignity. Take, for
example, the case reported in the *Evening Standard*:

> Five women teachers at the Parish Church Sunday
> School at Earls Barton, near Wellingborough, have
> been dismissed by the Vicar, the Revd L. A. Ewart,
> after a dispute about arrangements for the school's
> annual outing. A letter sent by Mr Ewart to Mrs
> H. Goode, another teacher, reads:
>   'One has enough to contend with in this Parish
> without battling against the whims of one or two
> Sunday School teachers.
>   'This revolutionary spirit will have a very bad
> effect on the Parish, and those who cause it will
> have to answer to God for their actions. Kneel
> down and ask God to guide you, and I know what
> the answer will be . . . It is ridiculous to think

of taking the children to Whipsnade. I have the
spiritual care of the Sunday School children in
Earls Barton. I cannot allow my authority to be
over-ridden. So I have dismissed the five teachers.'

It's a good job the teachers did not dare to suggest
that the children should be taken to Devon or
Cornwall, where 'henbane is growing wild', otherwise
they might have been burned at the stake. Those
counties, according to a spokesman from the West
Country Drugs Squad, issued this warning about the
aforesaid plant:

'We call it Devil-weed. People who take it as a
hot, tea-style drink, often turn into wild beasts or
spend weeks gazing at their television sets in a
state of dazed amazement.

'A local ice-porter held a long conversation with

a filing cabinet, a schoolteacher from St Ives said
that her class had been turned into pebbles on
the beach, and a local magistrate was found trying
to roll up the double yellow lines that had been
painted outside his home.'

It can be understood sometimes why teachers turn to
'hot tea with a touch of henbane' when they are reviled
in so many quarters. Sometimes, as in this letter in the
Daily Telegraph, the attack is pretty direct:

'Is it not time our teachers were told that their
job is not a profession, and that their attempt to
gang up with doctors, lawyers and others is an
impertinence.'
'The elementary schoolteacher is just a public
service employee, trained and paid at public cost,
and the job he does is very useful, but by no
means essential.'

Others are more subtle in their put down:

'Professor Alan Smithers, of Manchester
University's School of Education, said his survey of
young people showed that three main factors put
people off teaching – the pay, the status and the
children.
'He commented: "Teaching has never been a
very highly-paid profession. It is very difficult to
pay 400,000 teachers a lot more. It is important to
look for ways of targeting the money so that the
people who need it receive it."
'It was equally important,' he added, 'for the
Government to try to change the view that
teaching was a low-status profession."'

Things have got pretty bad when this can appear in the *Observer*:

> **'When the teacher is the only one in the
> classroom without a television, he can't help
> feeling his position.'**

Teachers, according to a wife writing in the *Teacher*, do not really need the wherewithal to live comfortably – their dedication should be sufficient to see them through:

> **'Her husband is a bank clerk and she herself
> loathes strikes. "Greed seems to take over," she
> said. "I know a teacher's job is an essential one
> – but when they talk about £100 a week, they
> mean take-home pay. Surely a teacher should be
> someone who can get most out of life without
> having to rely on money to do it."'**

Indeed, with such a pittance for a salary, one wonders how some teachers can manage at all.

> **It was gleefully reported in the H - - - - - Police
> Magazine that: 'PC Stout, on duty at Flamingo
> Park, came across a distressed boy who had
> accompanied his father, a teacher, on a school trip
> and had got lost. On being asked: "What's your
> Dad like?" PC Stout reported the boy's sobbing
> reply: "Beer, women and a Saturday bet."'**

The old maxim of 'Those who can, do; those who can't, teách', still holds strong. The question is, however, what *would* they have done if they could have?

Cruden's Complete Concordance on the Old and New Testaments (Lutterworth Press) cites the case of Alexander Cruden, who:

> '. . . was intended for the Presbyterian Ministry, but ill-health, which for a time affected his mind, led him to take up teaching at the age of 21.'

If this item from the *Observer Magazine* is to be believed, the general consensus of the status of teachers is such that, according to popular perception, there is no way other than up for even a Headteacher:

> 'The new British butler is typically a 45-year-old man who's been made redundant or had a business that's gone bust, or he's an ex-Headmaster . . .'

Junior and Secondary teachers can thank God that there are others in the teaching profession who come in for a lot of stick:

> 'I'm really disappointed with the calibre of people in this squat,' says Chris Welby, a Bassett Street squatter and a former student at Keele (writing in *New Society*). 'There's too much of what I'd call the teacher training college radical, not enough of the university radical. They're not quite up to taking the real opportunities.'

When you really get sick of teachers, you can 'hang 'em high', according to a notice in the cloakroom of the Sir John Cass School in the East End:

> 'These hooks are for teachers only.'
> To which someone had added:
> 'They may also be used for hats and coats.'

It is nice to see, from the *Guardian*, that not all teachers are considered to be at the bottom of the pile – well, that is if you happen to teach at our foremost public school:

> 'The Willow Tree is much favoured by Eton masters as well as by non-academic staff of the School and the local community. Mr Forster, who has been host of the Willow Tree for seven years, said that he did not want to leave, "because of the pleasantness of the masters, and there are some very nice normal folks here as well."'

Thereby hangs the rub – you have to be 'abnormal'.

The heart goes out to those in the profession who face hell and high water and then are thwarted at the very end of the day:

> 'Bert Barnett was a teacher,' writes the *Freethinker*, 'who never concealed his opposition to the statutory privileges enjoyed by Christianity in

the nation's schools. He formed what was probably
the first humanist group in a comprehensive
school. Although Mr Barnett had expressed a wish
to be cremated, we understand that he was buried
with a clergyman.'

For most of those who live to enjoy retirement, the
release from the daily grind can be exquisite. A retired
Head from Great Yarmouth recounted his first day of
real freedom:

'It was the first day back after the holidays, and I
lay there in bed. Outside I could hear the patter
of tiny feet and the sound of shrill voices as the
children made their way to school. I turned over
and, you know, I couldn't get to sleep . . . for
laughing.'

3
Letters

'*Bring a note in future!*' This phrase has been used by teachers from time immemorial, when any pupil has returned from absence without that formal piece of paper. What is being asked for is simply a few (truthful) words of explanation from a parent. In general, this is what teachers get, for most notes are bland in the extreme. There are, however, some interesting exceptions.

A Headteacher of a Huddersfield school recently received this missive from an exasperated but literate mother:

> '**Nicholas has had chicken-pox. He is now fully recovered, and I pass him back to your tender care, though why you want him all day is beyond me, as he has driven me to distraction during his confinement.**'

Other parents are far more protective of their off-spring. Such an attitude invariably does not extend to the children of others. A teacher in a Birmingham school realized this when she was sent this letter:

'Dear Miss,

If my darling Jessica May is in need of strictness
from you, will you shout at the child next to her
and that will be sufficient to upset her. Thank you
for your co-operation.

Yours sincerely,

Mrs F. Roberts'

Jessica May is obviously an adored child. But then, so
is Ricky, although they probably come from different
backgrounds. Ricky, by the way, is the subject of
this letter sent by a parent to the Headteacher of a
comprehensive school in Cornwall:

'Dear Sir,

Will you please give Ricky permission to ride his
TSx50 motorcycle to school? As Ricky doesn't like
to let his bike out of sight – he usually parks it in
his bedroom – can he please park it at the back of
the classroom?'

The reply is unknown, but presumably, whatever
Ricky wants, Ricky gets. Sheila, on the other hand,
didn't want cabbage, but continued to get it. As a
result, an Essex school reports receiving this anguished
note:

'Please don't force Sheila to take her helping of
cabbage at school meals. She just brings it home
every day stuffed down her socks!'

Most teachers can remember having received a letter
that has a clear ring of truth about it, even if it is not
expressed in the Queen's English. One feels for the
child who is the victim in this, and I am sure we all
wish him well:

> **'Dear Miss,**
>
> **I have not sent Johnny to school this morning
> because he hasn't been. I have given him something
> to make him go, and when he's been he'll come.'**

When you come to think about it, Shakespeare would
have been hard pushed to express the situation in a
more forceful and illuminating way.

Toilet habits, in fact, often form the subject matter
of notes to school. One such example is the letter to
a teacher which read:

> **'Dear Miss,**
>
> **Please excuse Sandra being late. She was waiting**

> for the bus at twenty to nine, but came back to use
> the toilet and missed it.'

Oh, dear!

But excuses for absence can be categorized . . . into
the downright 'uncompromising':

> 'Owen did not attend your detention yesterday
> because I told him not to, and he is more
> frightened of me than he is of you.'

. . . into the 'Sorry, I'll say that again':

> 'Kevin was off one day last week as he played
> truant, and I kept him off for the rest of the week
> as I was frightened he would do it again.'

. . . into 'physical impossibilities':

> 'I'm sorry Michael could not attend school
> yesterday, but I was hanging on to the mantelpiece
> with my stomach.'
>   'Sorry George could not make it to school
> yesterday, as the house is being decorated and I
> was upside down with the painter.'

'Donald has been away with his head. He has had it on and off all week.'

'Please allow Brian not to take games for a few months – the doctor says he has an airline fracture in his left shin.'

'Ashley has been off school because I have had the baby. It was not his fault.'

and finally, the category of 'Not Guilty, m'Lord!':

'Veronica was absent with permission because her sister had a baby. Please thank the Headmaster.'

Some parents collude with their child's absence from school in a sophisticated and plausible manner. Some of the excuses used are so ingenious that they deserve to be accepted at face value. Thus the Headteacher of a Grantham school was rendered speechless by this letter:

> 'Dear Sir,
>
> Paul was late because while he was waiting for the bus, he heard the national anthem on the radio. While he stood to attention the bus went by and he had to catch a later one.'

On the other hand, other parents have long since done with excuses, however clever these might be. A school in Kent wrote to one home, enquiring why a boy had not attended. This was the reply:

> 'Shane his not Ben to shool Be co's he ant Ben for one year and I carnt see wy he has to come aney more Beco'se he Dont wont to come back aneymore so I ant sending him.'

Well, you carnt sey farrer than that, I surpose.

Most note-writers want to support their child's school and write humbly and helpfully to explain a situation, even if things do not quite turn out as intended. This letter to a Somerset school is in this category:

> 'Dear Madam,
>
> I am just writing to confirm that Katie was not at school yesterday because my wife entered her in a pony competition (she came second).'

Far less supportive, and much more aggressive, however, is this note to the Headteacher of a Doncaster comprehensive school:

> 'Dear Mr Smith,
>
> My son should not be kept behind after class as I do

not approve of the French language. English is the
only language he needs to know. Thanking you.'

A case of 'Parlez vous Doncastrian', I suppose. Then
there was this letter from an irate mother in London:

'Dear Madam,

Please ixcuse Tommy today. He wont come to
scule becos he is acting as a time-keeper for his
father & it's all yore fault. You ask if a field is 6
miles round how long can a man going at 3 miles
an hour walk twice round it. Tommy aint a man
so we had to send his father. They went early this
morning and father will walk and Tommy time him.
But please dont do this again as my husband must
work every day to support his family.'

When you think about it, who can blame her?

Not that all the letters emanating from schools
are examples of deathless prose. A Junior school in
Nottingham sent these rather ambiguous words home
with its young charges:

'Your child has been selected for cooking. Please
send 50p towards the cost . . .'

and from a school in Rugby:

'I am sorry that we are unable to offer a place
to Jimmy for inclusion on the ski course at this
late stage. The problem we have is the flight is
completely full but if someone drops out, as is often
the case, we shall contact you immediately.'

4

Apocryphal/ Miscellaneous

Staff rooms are full of stories about things children have said – or gaffs that colleagues have made. Such yarns enter into a school's folklore, and are given new life when recounted to each newcomer. Just as such bonhomie saved soldiers in the two World Wars from going under with the strain of events, so this tale-telling has had a similar function as teachers have tottered under the barrage of the national curriculum, appraisal, OFSTED inspection, and so on.

Talking of inspection, during a review of a northern primary school's religious education provision, it is said that an HMI, wishing to gauge a class's grasp of the New Testament, asked the question:

> **'Who was born in a stable and went on to have an influence throughout the World?'**
> **One girl nervously raised her hand, and in a hushed tone asked: 'Please, sir, was it Red Rum?'**

Many years earlier, an adviser went into a school whose Headteacher was well known for his ignorance.

> The adviser also asked a question. This time it was: 'Who wrote Hamlet?' One boy cheekily replied: 'Well, it wasn't me!' The adviser was suitably amused, and having established the boy's name as Tompkins, told the Head of the incident. The Head laughed uproariously for a time, and then said: 'Don't you believe it. That Tompkins can't be trusted with anything. I bet it was him all the time.'

Religious education, perhaps unsurprisingly, forms a rich source of ignorance on the part of pupils. A GCSE Board's *Annual Report* gives this quote from an aspiring student's paper:

> 'Christ cured Peter's wife's mother, when she was sick of a fever, and Peter cursed and swore and went out and wept bitterly.'

Unlikely to become the next Archbishop of Canterbury ...!

A 14-year-old girl at a Surrey comprehensive school finds herself blessed with the gift of brevity:

> Given up to 30 minutes in a religious education examination to tackle the question: 'Was it lawful to buy or sell on the Sabbath day?' she replied simply: 'Buy!' This gave her 29 minutes and 45 seconds to read through her answer and make any corrections to spelling she felt necessary.

Meanwhile, at a Sunday School only 30 miles away

in Willesden, a teacher said to her class of five-year-olds:

> 'That's the story of Jonah and the whale. What does it teach us?' After a bemused silence, a boy piped up from the back: 'Please, Miss, that you can't keep a good man down!'

This boy, with his healthy scepticism, must have a relative at the other end of the country, in Wigtownshire:

> Here a seven-year-old girl was forced, under duress, to go to her younger brother's end-of-term carol concert. After much arguing, she got to the school, and at the door was given some money by her mother to put in the collection plate. To this, she piped up loudly for all to hear: 'You don't mean to say that we have to pay for this as well?'

Interviews are always trying, and none more so than

for the candidate for a general teaching post in
Durham:

> He had written on his application form under
> 'Qualifications': BA (Oxon), only to be greeted with
> the well-meant remark: 'I see you have a degree in
> agriculture.'

A similar story comes from Manchester.

> The candidate's application form for a business
> studies post was being carefully scrutinized by a
> local councillor. The candidate had worked, as
> he had indicated, for some years in FE. When
> the time arrived for 'any further questions', the
> councillor asked:
> 'Did you enjoy teaching physical education, then?'

Teachers aspiring to promotion often feel that the
tension of the interview does not allow them to give
of their best. Others go to pieces completely. Those
who have been through such fraught experiences can
empathize with the poor teacher who was seeking a
maths post in North Yorkshire:

> 'When the interview was over, he was thanked
> and asked to wait in an adjoining room. He began
> to leave, but instead of choosing the exit door, he
> chose the adjacent toilet door. Those interviewing
> did not have a chance to stop him, and when he did
> not come back out immediately they assumed he
> was answering the call of nature. After 15 minutes,
> it was clear all was not well, and when the Head
> gingerly pushed the door open, there was the
> unfortunate candidate riveted, panic-stricken, with
> arms outsplayed against the wall.'

At least that candidate did fill in and send off his application form, thereby giving himself a chance – which is more than can be said for a hopeful from Stirling:

> After advertising a post, a Headteacher received an envelope containing a scrap of paper, which read:
> 'I lb. of butter (not salted), I pkt of digestives, 2 doz. eggs . . .'
> Obviously, some time later in Tesco or Safeway a would-be applicant was pulling out of his carrier a shopping list that read:
> 'I have attended many courses . . .'

As befits their qualifications, teachers often display a clear and instinctive intelligence. Like the staff at a Bristol comprehensive school, for example:

> This school was swiftly going to rack and ruin because of an outbreak of offensive graffiti. The perpetrator, however, always got away with it by getting up to his tricks at night. One day, staff returned to find written on a toilet wall the words:
> 'I have vandillised here befor meny times.'
> They swiftly gave all suspects a spelling test, which included the words: 'vandillised', 'befor' and 'meny'. The one boy who got these wrong also got six months youth custody.

Pupils in Year 7 at a school in Camberwell were once asked to write an essay on the harmful effects of oil on sea life. One response was thus:

> 'When my mum opened a tin of sardines last night, it was full of oil and all the sardines were dead.'

Another boy, asked to write on how to encourage motorists to show more consideration to others, gave a short answer:

'Drive a police car.'

Just because it's short, of course, doesn't mean to say it's wrong.

It is a common misconception that all pupils want to do is play about and hinder the teacher. Often the reverse is true. All they want to do is help, but their enthusiasm can be open to misinterpretation.

An art class at a Stockton school was more restless than usual. When finally asked what the matter was, a boy raised his hand and said:

'Please, Sir, your jacket's on fire!'
The art teacher lost his temper, and attacked the youth for being so cheeky. Some minutes later, the teacher's jacket burst into flames. Unfortunately for him, he'd left a lit cigarette in the pocket!

There is a similar tale to this, but with the shoe firmly on the other foot. A teacher in Wanstead met an ex-pupil, then aged about 30, in the High Street one Saturday.

The ex-pupil had with him his wife and three children. Pleasantries were exchanged and the ex-pupil kept his hand in his pocket throughout these exchanges, seemingly oblivious of the smoke that was billowing out. The teacher then made an excuse and left, but as he looked back, he saw the husband dogging out a cigarette on the ground and saying to his wife: 'I don't think he noticed!'

Such is the fear the teaching profession holds over its unfortunate victims!

Indeed, to some pupils, the teacher is like God, seen everywhere. This is especially so for the child in a Buckinghamshire primary school.

> Her teacher was talking about numbers, times and clocks. The question was then asked: 'What has two arms, a face, and keeps telling you something?'
> After a pause, the girl asked: 'Do you spell "Teacher" with one 'e' or two?'

In general, though, pupils tend not to be overawed by authority, and good luck to them for that.

> One boy, when once asked by his teacher, the tense of the sentence 'I am beautiful', replied, without a moment's hesitation:
> 'Past tense, Miss!'

Even more to the point was the comment by the girl from a Cheshire School.

> She and her classmates went to London, visited the Houses of Parliament, and were entertained on the Members' terrace as the sun sank majestically in the west over the Thames. 'What do you think of this?' said her teacher, awe-struck by the magnificence of it all. The 13-year-old sipped from her cup thoughtfully, and then said: 'This tea's a bit strong!'

A future prime minister in the making, no doubt!

5
Misspellings and Mistakes

Frequently, whether because of the pressure to meet deadlines, or out of pure mischievousness, the efforts of reporters produce gaffs which can make their readers squirm with delight, while they do likewise, but with embarrassment. What else but untold pressure could have prompted a reporter on the *Birmingham Evening Mail* to concoct the following headline:

**Slimming disease
girl, 15, vanishes**

That comes into the same category as the following headline from the *Salisbury Journal*, though perhaps on this occasion the writer was a very devout anti-cleric:

**Top-hated
Bishop stole
the show at
School Fête**

Occasionally part of one newspaper item becomes inextricably entangled with another to produce an incomprehensible, but nevertheless enjoyable, piece of information. Such an example was contained in an Essex paper, and states:

> 'Three girls gained State Scholarships which took them to B——————College, and at 25p per lb. are of excellent quality.'

And was this young musician performing on his bike . . . ?

> 'Fourteen-year-old Victor Harris has passed with credit two of the recent Royal Academy of Music piano examinations. For failing to stop he was fined £5.'
>
> *(Darlington & Stockton Times)*

There are times when the obvious escapes the speaker who cannot see the 'wood for the trees' – or is it, as in this case, the 'toes for the ankles' . . . ?

> 'We want to produce dancers who at 16 can walk into the Royal Ballet School, or any other national ballet school and stand on their own two feet.'
>
> *(Daily Telegraph)*

Sometimes the feeling is that it only makes matters worse when an apology is made, and it would have been better to let the world go by instead of seeking redress, as in this case from the *Daily Express*:

> 'We are asked to point out that Mr Gerry Waites,

**father of Miss Jennifer Waites, whose attendance at
a Buckingham Palace Brownie party was reported
in yesterday's *Daily Express*, is the public relations
officer to the Gulf Oil company, Great Britain, and
not a plumber, as was stated in error.'**

It is fairly common for those involved in – or on the
peripheries of – education, to go to the extreme when
they consider the question of punishment. Typical is
this report on an education speech from the *Newcastle
Journal*:

**'Capital punishment to the wrong type of child –
the nervous, sensitive type – may do irreparable
harm,' he said.**

Well, there should certainly be unanimity of agreement on that one.

But have some schools been getting away with
murder? A report in the *Harrow Independent* implies
that they have:

**'Motions calling for the temporary suspension of
capital punishment in Harrow's Middle and High
Schools were on the Agenda for the Meeting of
the Borough Education Committee on Tuesday
evening.'**

It would seem, however, that parents support this
tough approach:

**'10.30 Thames Report: Is the ILEA, which has
banned capital punishment in its schools, flying in**

the face of parents' wishes? They say they prefer it
to continue.'

The assumption has always been that many of the public
would have at least shot, hanged or electrocuted pupils
in schools where 'capital punishment' was favoured.
The *Leamington Spa Observer*, however, hints that,
in that part of suburbia, cannibalism appears to be
'in vogue':

> 'ERROR
> The *Observer* wishes to apologize for a typesetting
> error in our "Tots and Toddlers" advertising
> feature last week which led to Binswood Nursery
> School being described as serving "children
> casserole" instead of "chicken casserole".'

In Cambridge at least, they are more traditional in the
execution of their duties:

> **Teachers**
> **Hang Five**
> **Over**
> **Action**

As the *Harrow Observer* would indicate if death is good
enough for the pupils, why should it not be for the
teachers? – *à la guillotine.*

> 'The staff of a Kenton School is to be cut despite
> the fact that it will have more pupils. St Joseph's
> Infant School will lose half a teacher.'

From time to time the *Times Educational Supplement*

throws up a gem which can not surely be anything other than intentional – or is it?

**Labour Whip
Opposes Cane**

What are we to make of this headline . . . ?

**Headteacher, father of nine,
fined £100 for not stopping.**

Commentators on dyslexia have been known to make the odd mistake, again as can be seen from the *Daily Telegraph*:

**Music As Help
in Dyslexia**

by John Izbicki, Education Correspondent

'King's College Choir School, Cambridge, is to put to the test a theory that children who suffer from ear, nose or throat infection in infancy are likely to experience difficulty in learning to read and become "word glind".'

. . . and from the *Darlington and Stockton Times*:

'Monday's spring sunshine and the cheerful endorsement of Susan Hampshire put the seal of success on a project in Darlington. Miss Hampshire, often described as the best-known dyslexic in Britainm was in town for the formal opening of the dyslexia teaching centre at Cockerton Methodist Church Hall.'

From time to time the inclusion of a single number can alter the whole perception of the inhabitants of a school. This one from the *Bristol Evening Post* inspires visions of walking sticks, beards and short trousers:

> **'The XIV Century School is housed in Druid Stoke House, Druid Stoke Avenue, and currently has a roll of 80 boys between 7 and 103, although it does take a few boys from the age of 5.'**

It must be regretted that, according to this newspaper from Grantham, the education of the pensioners is going to be stifled as a result of the shortening of hours:

> **'The children in the Junior School start at 8.50 a.m. and finish at 4 p.m. If this arrangement continues next year, the eighty-year-olds who will remain in the first school will lost 3 hours 20 minutes a week of schooling.'**

Who could not feel pity for this man whose death was reported in the *Grauniad*:

**'Maths inventor Edward Begle, innovator of the
"New Maths" taught to millions of youngsters, has
died from emphysema and California.'**

. . . and to think he thought the climate would be good
for his health!

State schools have long provided an excellent scape-
goat for all the various wrongs of the world, from
the rise in juvenile delinquency to the fall in general
educational standards. Journalists in particular, when
they are short of copy, can always fill a few column
inches by complaining about learning (or the lack
of it!) in the secondary sector. Pots can, however,
call kettles black, as this report from the *Financial
Times* proves:

**'Employers in the commercial sector have voiced
their concern over low education standards.
Their argument that standards of grammer are
holding back industrial progress were greeted with
sympathy in parlaiment yesterday.'**

'Grammar', or 'grammer', as it is often known is a
lovely word. The difficulty that many people find in
spelling it is one of the best possible reasons for doing
away with our 'grammer' schools. 'Comprehensive'
may be over twice as long, but at least it doesn't
pose the same problems. This point should be made,
perhaps, in the next session of 'parlaiment'.

Employers, when their profits fall, also like to take
a swipe at schools. The fact that pupils at 16 cannot
understand calculus or analyse *King Lear* is often

used as reasons why our balance of payments is in the red.

There are, however, some advantages in illiteracy. Those who cannot read won't know what is wrong with this advertisement:

**Required by Dublin-based
market research company**

**SCHOOL LEVER
Male/Femaly**

Those who can read, on the other hand, won't know what is right with another advertisement, found in the *Times Higher Educational Supplement*, which went as follows:

Kingston Polytechnic

Applications are invited for the post of

RDFDJRCH ASSISTANT

**to work on numerical mdomods in ovtimum
design problems**

On second thoughts, perhaps the job is so complex that this is exactly what they do want. In which case:

**Dear Sir/Madam,
Jkhgf yutrs lpnb . . .**

In fairness, it is not only employers and journalists who are horrified at the decline in standards from what they was like in our day. University admissions officers have a similar concern. The *Daily Telegraph* reports with abhorrence on these new trends:

'The tutors also complain of many sixth-form candidates who appear at interviews in open-neck shirts, and whose aplications fomrs abound in spelling mistakes.'

Can't do much about the open-necked shirts, I'm afraid, but the *Rhymney Valley Express* offers some hope on the spelling. Or does it?

Mid Glamorgan Adult
Literacy/Numeracy
Service

For help with:

Reading Spelling
Aritimetic

It certainly wouldn't be any good for the staff of a primary school in Oxfordshire to go there for help. They wrote to their local bookshop, asking for ...

'... a diagnostic and Remedial Spelling Manuel plus a Teacher's Manuel.'

They could try this advertisement in the *Wiltshire Times* – at least the advertiser can spell, even if the grammar is a bit suspect:

'Does your child need extra extra tuition with their English. I'm a graduate English teacher with experience. Ring ...'

I wonder if his name is 'Manuel' ...?
Finally – this erratum appeared in an Avon *Governors' Newsletter*:

SPECIAL EDUCATIONAL NEEDS

Rather than refer to 'the reasonable person (generally the Head)', it should have said: 'the responsible person'.

Clearly an error – for when was any Head *ever* reasonable . . . ?

6

Administration

The administration in our education establishments, whether by LEAs, governors, headteachers, or sometimes caretakers, frequently demonstrates a madness and bureaucracy which stifles initiative and good management.

> 'Who will forget the basketball match in North Shields, which was coming to an exciting conclusion. Both sides were on level points, and the ball was hurtling towards the net in the dying seconds, when the basket and its structure began to move. It was 9.30 p.m., and the caretaker's contract clearly stipulated that all activities must end at that precise moment.'

School meals have always been the subject of childhood memories in which the lingering smell of boiled cabbage has taken its place alongside wax polish and overburdened toilets. Children of a school in Bridgend, according to the *Daily Mail*, will have no memories of the corned beef which was sent to their school canteen.

'Teachers sniffed it and did not like it. A Canteen Manageress sniffed it, but pronounced it good; the Town Sanitary Inspector sniffed it, and passed it as good; the Town Medical Officer sniffed it, and declared it good – then ordered it to be destroyed, because too many people had sniffed it!'

It makes one wonder what the health authorities would make of these reports which have appeared in British newspapers:

'Dunnington parents plan to use packed lunches as ammunition in their campaign to get their children back into schools at lunch times.'

(Worksop Guardian)

'Dr T. H. Sanderson-Wells, Food Education Society Chairman, told in London yesterday of a perfectly balanced chemical meal, containing all the necessary vitamins, which was fed to a number of rats. They all died.'

(Daily Mail)

'The milk supplied to Lanarkshire schools is excellent. There may be an odd bottle with a beetle or snail in it, but that won't do you any harm.'

It must, however, be comforting for parents north of the Border to know that, when their children do finally succumb, they will do so on holiday, released from academic pressures. A report in the *Scottish Daily Express* carries the information that:

> '"In the event of a nuclear attack, children will be given a day off school," says the Scottish Home and Health Department.'

Education Authorities and Officers can frequently be prime examples of how the 'law is an ass' in the application of their regulations.

> The Gough Family became only too aware of this when their eight-year-old daughter, Pauline, was too old to be given permission by local officials to share an otherwise empty taxi, which calls at the house for her seven-year-old sister, Sheila:
> 'It has been decreed' reports the *News Chronicle*, 'that Pauline will have to walk the five and a half miles along lonely lanes to and from school.'

From time to time the perspicacity shown by education officials is breathtaking, as can be seen from the response to one parent's action attempting to make life safer for the pupils of one school:

> 'In reply to her protests and petition, the Ministry of Transport also says that the employment of a school crossing patrol is unwarranted, as it would be used by children.'
>
> (*Evening Standard*)

Bureaucracy is a wonderful thing – where would we

be without it? Quite a long way, if this report from the *Guardian* is anything to go by. It reports that the former Department of Education once sent a circular to every education authority in the country, instructing them on how to make holes in walls, so that they could hang pictures.

> **'A wall,' went the circular, 'is a rectangle with horizontal and vertical sides.'**

Still on the subject of bureaucracy, the story is told of a local inspector trying to find his way to a well-thought-of comprehensive located among a maze of back and side streets. After what seemed an eternity of failing to find the school, the inspector stopped the car, rolled down the window, and asked a nine-year-old urchin:

> **'Could you tell me how to get to St Michael's, please?'**
> **'My Mam says if you behave yourself and work really hard, you might have a chance!' was the eloquent reply.**

He found his way – as presumably did this one, eventually:

> **The inspector stopped and asked a policeman for directions to Guisborough Teachers' Centre, where he was to attend a meeting.**
> **'Straight ahead at the next lights, first left, then first right, Sir.'**
> **The Inspector thanked him, and off he sped.**
> **Four hours later, the meeting ended, the inspector was returning, when he saw the same**

policeman standing in the same spot. Unable to
resist the temptation, he rolled down the window
and shouted across:
  'Officer – you did say "first left", didn't you?'

Central government directions of a different nature
are often so complex that they are rendered useless:

The financing of local government in England, issued
by the Department of the Environment, carried
this formula to be used to calculate the allowance
for students crossing local authority boundaries for
their education:

$$\frac{(V \times 1.36 \times W \times 1.114)}{X + (Y \times 0.36)} \ (+0.917 \times 2 \times 1.126)$$

Not much scope for manoeuvre with that, so it is
refreshing to be given the option and flexibility which
was offered in *Administrative Memorandum 48* from
the Ministry of Education:

'The attendance register must be marked at the
beginning of each morning or afternoon session
during the time set apart for registration in the
timetable. During this time every pupil whose name
has been entered in and not removed from the
Admission Registers must be marked \ (present) or
O (absent). (It is of course open to schools to make
the marks from left to right or from right to left
according to individual convenience.)'

From time to time there is evidence to suggest that
pupils are seen by LEAs not as human beings, but
merely as numbers on a computer. Mr Herbert Coles,

of Armour Valley School, complained that the Local Education Authority had failed to provide a warden to assist children across a nearby road:

> **'The last time they turned us down,' he said, 'was on the grounds that the warden's life would be in danger from passing cars.'**

Sometimes it can be equally as dangerous sitting on a school committee reviewing the Local Management of Schools budget, according to one chairman, who said he did not want a repetition of the farce that occurred on the last occasion. He said:

> **'A lot of sand was thrown in our eyes. This time we want something more concrete.'**

In an age when our young people are exposed to all sorts of external pressures which can have such profound effects upon their behaviour, it is comforting to know that the guardians of our moral welfare are keeping a keen eye on the dangers presented by the modern cinema. Parents in the North-East can rest easy at night, having been informed by the *News Chronicle* that:

> **'A showing of *Snow White and the Seven Dwarfs* will be given at a Durham cinema tomorrow for the city magistrates to decide whether the film is fit for children unaccompanied by adults.'**

Technology is always in the news these days. Not long ago, if a person could plug in a computer and switched it on, then he was a technologist. Times have changed, and it appears a title needs to match the complexities of the subject. The *Northampton Evening Telegraph* carried this information:

> '**Mr T. G. Fendick, Education Officer for the Isle, has been appointed representative of the Isle Education Committee to serve on the Area Technological Sub-Committee for the Western Area of the East Anglian Regional Advisory Council for Further Education.**'

It is hoped he will have the opportunity to develop his plans without the attentions of this type of commentator reported in the *Times Educational Supplement*:

> '**The former chairman of the governors, Mr J. Claricoats, is said to have asked: "If it is called Enfield College of Technology, why have we got all these art courses?" Another remark by the same man has reverberated round the corridors of Enfield: "Social Science, social work, sociology, socialism, it's all the same thing, isn't it?"**'

From time to time local dignitaries show they have the education of the children in their localities at heart. The *Sunday Despatch* informs us:

> '**To get sufficient ball-boys for South of England Lawn Tennis Championships, Eastbourne Entertainments Committee asks for longer secondary school holidays.**'

Governors, too, have a disinclination to concentrate their minds on those things which are at the centre of child development. The *Sunday Express* reports that the governors of Fishguard (Pembs.) County School are divided on the question of bare-legged teachers.

> **Said one governor (a man):**
>   'Pupils have to wear stockings, but teachers go with bare legs. There can be no discipline.'

The demands in standards and targets expected by inspectors of teachers and pupils do not always extend to the Local Education Authorities. A letter to all educational establishments in Hertfordshire contained this paragraph:

> 'Visits to sites by contractors tendering for grounds maintenance work . . . are to enable the contractors to quantify and price the work they will be asked to do, and I would ask you particularly not to persuade contractors that a higher standard of grounds maintenance than has traditionally been achieved should now be aimed for. The specification is intended to reflect current standards, since those standards are what can currently be afforded.'

It might have been expected that a County English adviser could be relied upon to communicate accurately, but this extract from his letter to Heads of English Departments casts doubts upon that capacity:

> 'From the replies to my letter . . . it is evident now that enough schools will be unable to release their Heads of English to make this Conference unviable. It will therefore not take place.'

Presumably the following materials were similarly superfluous to needs, even before being rounded up and deposited in far away lands:

'OBSOLETE TEXTBOOKS COLLECTED AND SENT ABROAD

Obsolete textbooks are being collected by the Education Committee from the Authority's schools, and sent to the English-Speaking Union, 37 Charles Street, London W1, for distribution to Commonwealth Countries where they are urgently needed.'

Often it must be a boring and thankless task working as a clerk in administration, but this one at least clearly and legitimately enjoys his extra-curricular activities. Giving an interview in the *Evening Standard*, he reports:

'"I'm a clerk during the daytime," he said. "At night I keep an eye on excessive drinking and loose-living in the West End."

"Another part of my job is to buy and read obscene novelettes from the doorway stalls which appear in the West End at nights, I mark the objectionable bits and send them to the Council."

"That, and watching the nude shows in the small suburban theatres or patrolling the parks, keeps me busy in my spare nights."

"No, I don't get any pay for it. Just my expenses." '

Practical experience can clearly bring job satisfaction, but not in the way suggested by Edinburgh's Director of Education, reported in the *Sunday Express*:

'Teachers noticed a new look in children's eyes after an experimental sex education course.'

Although administrative jobs may not be the most exciting in the world, secretarial posts in schools are much sought after. Among a batch of applications made to a school in Melrose were these two comments:

'I have worked in the crisp factory for nine years now and think it is time to move on.'

And what is one to make of this applicant's information . . . ?

'I am also familiar with a number of the teachers.'

7

Pupils – Bad, Good, Indifferent and Royal

There is no doubt that some parents cannot accept that their offspring are capable of misconduct, while they assume that the progeny of other couples are naturally inclined towards evil. A typical case of *'My son, my son can do no wrong'* can be seen in this story carried by the *Birmingham Post*:

> 'I was with Ian when he was at the Club. He is not uncontrollable. He is big, but then boys are bigger than girls. None of the other mothers complained to me. Ian did shut Mrs Carter's little girl in a trunk. He's a naturally tidy child, and puts all things away.'

Bullying is one thing, but things are definitely getting out of hand when pupils resort to the attempted murder of their teacher. This story, carried in *The Times*, says little for the acquisition of spiritual values at a public school, and perhaps even less for the quality of food:

'Council said, according to Pamela Haytor, the
attitude of these girls towards their mistresses
seemed to have been unsatisfactory. On one
occasion there had been talk of poisoning Miss
Davis, one of the mistresses. Not having any rat
poison, metal polish and disinfectant were sprinkled
in her soup.'

Some pupils, it would appear from the *News of the
World*, have become amoral at a very early age.

It is reported that two 12-year-olds asked, at the
Juvenile Court at Wimbledon, London, if they were
sorry for wrecking a hall. Both replied: 'Yes, we
thought it was the Church we were breaking up!'

Lack of morality may engender vandalism, but from
time to time the accused will search frantically for
an explanation of criminal misconduct. This was

borne out in a report in the *Evening Standard* of an incident in which a 16-year-old Acton boy admitted being drunk and disorderly while on a coach trip to Southend.

> '"I think it was the ice cream that made me aggressive!" he excused himself gastronomically as he was fined £2.00. The citizens of Southend should thank God he did not have whipped cream in addition, or that might have been an end of their pier . . . !'

The nerve of some youths knows no bounds as seen from the *Sidcup and Kentish Times*, which reported . . .

> . . . a policeman informing the Court that, apart from the incidents which led to their arrest, 'the boys had been in the habit of taking cars and driving in them to visit their probation officers.'

Sheer impertinence is not only limited to those for whom the bus is not good enough. This snippet from the *Gloucestershire Echo* takes a bit of beating for cheek:

> 'After a school lesson demonstrating the value of money, a nine-year-old girl stole £1.12 of the cash used in the demonstration.'

The demonstrator had cause to feel aggrieved, as had the parkkeeper reported in the *Bexhill-on-Sea Observer*. The local council followed Home Office advice and installed unbreakable glass in the cricket pavilion. A young hooligan hurled a brick at the window, which failed to break. The brick re-bounded and struck him a severe blow on the foot.

> **'I think it is criminal that the council should put such materials in their buildings,' the irate mother complained to the surprised custodian.**

It is heartening at least to be aware that some of our criminals do have a sense of sartorial standards when they finally arrive in the dock. The *Lincolnshire Echo* reported:

> **'A youth stole a shirt from Littlewoods, Lincoln, so that he could look smart when he appeared in Court the next day, the City Magistrates were told.'**

It would appear, from a story in *The Times*, that once sentenced, the criminal element are never satisfied. Arthur Brazier, aged 18, told Wolverhampton magistrates that he absconded from a borstal institution because life was too easy.

> **'There is no discipline at all,' he commented, 'and I started getting relaxed and idle. That's the reason I ran away.' He added; 'The taxpayer ought to find out about this.'**

Who said the youth of today were not public spirited . . . ?

With such citizen-concern and the following type of eagle-eyed perspicacity from our local policemen, can there really be an increase in unsolved crime? The *Birmingham Evening Mail* reports:

> **'Police sergeant Victor Gillings thought it suspicious**

the night in Solihull just before Christmas, when he saw one of two children carrying a sign under his arm, saying "BETHLEHEM". As he told Solihull magistrates: "I was certain about the sign. When I was overseas I was stationed at a place called Bethlehem, and I knew there was no place of that name in this locality." '

At times we may ask whether the magistrates display a touch of misguided patriotism:

'A broken knife was produced at Clerkenwell when two youths appeared before Mr Pope, charged with shop-breaking. "Why don't you buy a British knife?" Mr Pope asked them. "You had better buy British if you are going in for burglary. This one is no earthly use!" '

Schools do have, of course, the professional and practical guidance of the psychologists who can give hope in apparently hopeless cases, as witnessed by this report in the *Ross-shire Journal*:

'Miss Georgina P. Mathie, principal psychologist, County of Stirling, quoted the case of a nine-year-old boy who ran amok with a hatchet in the large family of which he was a member, saying: "There are far too many bairns here." She showed how, by psychological treatment, he became completely adjusted, and several years later, was working a guillotine in a printer's establishment.'

This does demonstrate that, when you do find a child interested in something, in this case sharp instruments, *your* troubles might well be over (but they're only just beginning for someone else . . . !).

At the end of the day, teachers know that they can, in *prima facie* cases, rely on the co-operation of concerned parents – or can they? There would appear to be some doubt after reading this extract from the *Oxford Mail*:

> 'The boy's parents said he was suspended after a series of incidents at the school in which he squirted sodium hydroxide in a pupil's face, used a chisel on a girl's hand, and melted plastic beakers on a stove.
>
> The suspension angered the parents, who claim it was excessive and unjust. They say they have spoken to people involved in the incidents, and have been assured that their son was not acting with malice.'

Perhaps it is just as well that parents do support their children, right or wrong, or else the same thing might happen to them as Christine's Mam and Dad, as reported in the *Los Angeles Times*:

> 'Because they complained when Tootsie, her pet rabbit, soiled their living room carpet, 14-year-old Miss Christine Martin picked up the family handgun and shot her parents to death. During her interview she said:
>
> "I have been having problems with them for some time."'

Miss Martin appears a little mixed up, as does this man – or is it woman? – in the *News of the World*:

'I went through that ghastly adolescent phase most
girls experience. I went from child to woman in one
go. One day I was a child. The next a man.'

Now that is a case of schizophrenia which could lead
to problems, but what excuse have these children in
the *Chicago Times?*

'"The fete began very well," said Mrs Barbara
Picton, Headteacher of Blestow School.
    "The infants gathered around the Reverend
Harper and went: Baaa! . . . Baaa! . . . as they
played pageant sheep.

'"But when they had to become Vikings and raid
the Church, I am afraid they rather overdid things.
They hit Reverend Harper over the head with his
crook, and carried off the gold cup from the altar.
It took me twenty minutes to get the cup back."'

Violence of a different nature befell Mrs Osborne,
living in the area of the *Orpington and Petts Wood
News Shopper.*

'"The boys started to leave," she said. "Shortly after, I heard a noise in my front garden. I rushed out to find the plastic gnome in my front garden had been beaten up, and left lying on the path. The boys had gone." All things being considered, it's been a bad year for Mrs Osborne's gnomes. Her entire "family" of them was stolen in summer. Now a replacement has been beaten up.'

It was clearly a mistake, as reported in the *Belfast Telegraph*, to pack 1,000 schoolchildren into the Ritz Cinema one morning to show them a series of films dealing with road safety. Indeed, a fatal mistake, if finer feelings were expected:

'The children's reaction to the pictures was worthy of note. They cheered the accidents and laughed when an elderly cyclist wobbling over the road caused a collision, ending in the death of one boy and the maiming of another.'

Such behaviour unfortunately does give ammunition

for this balanced and sensitive type of letter which appeared in the *Daily Express*:

> **'Man is the lowest of the animals, especially those of the so-called working class.**
>
> **As for "little children", these are mostly vicious, thieving, destructive pests – you want to go to live in the Hammersmith or North Kensington area and you will soon find this out for yourself.'**

But why should pupils be insulted by the public when their teachers can do it perfectly well in reports? A small selection suffices to highlight their caustic wit:

> **'Tim's cheerful smile will get him through most things in life, but not, I fear, the 'O' level maths exam.'**
>
> **'His mind is like unto a muddy pond in which occasionally gleams a goldfish.'**

> **'This boy is not only off the rails, but half-way down the embankment as well.'**

> **'Marvin has leadership qualities – the class will
> follow him anywhere, if only out of curiosity . . .'**
> **'The only thing Harry has ever taken up at school
> has been space.'**

Then, of course, there was the metalwork pupil
who . . .

> **'. . . if you give him the job, he will finish the tools.'**

The new movement towards self-assessment reporting
has thrown up some interesting comments:

> **'I think I have iproved in Scince and Engolish. I
> need to iprove my spilling.'**

The heartfelt wish of this young lad combines the
physical and the academic:

> **'My ambition is to be taller and neater by the
> fourth year.'**

There is no doubt that one of the ways to ensure 'the
devil does not make work for idle hands' is to provide
exciting choices for our young people. The *Leamington
Spa Courier* carried this letter from a well-meaning,
but frustrated, local:

> **'These days we hear so much of what we should do
> to keep the young generation off the street corners,
> but when there is an event arranged and advertised
> for them, it is poorly patronized.
>   Such an occasion happened this week at Harbury,
> when a beetle drive was organized by the Village
> Hall Trust.'**

Even the search to find out the reasons for juvenile uninterest prove fruitless, as reported in the *Telegraph and Argos*:

> **'Despite a £25 first prize for 1,000 word essay competition on "Why Young People are so Apathetic", no entries have been received.'**

Children really can let down the teacher. A nervous probationer read in horror the results of a survey conducted by one inspector in her class, as reported in the *Irish Times*:

> **'The survey showed that, in a class of 21, not one pupil knew what marmalade was, and a sixth-class pupil who saw horses being fed with nose bags, on a school tour, thought they were sniffing glue.'**

Confusion can be the result of inexperience, and very few seem to be as confused as this gentleman described in the *Nairobi Standard*:

> **'The key witness said that he had gone to school for only one day, but had learned to speak English in the bars. He said that was in 1966, and he had been born in 1956. He said he was then twenty years old. Asked why there was a discrepancy, Wachira Ndirang said that, although he had learned to speak English in bars, he had not had the opportunity to learn mathematics.'**

Even culture is now being curbed by Health and Safety considerations, lest our young ones come to grief:

> **'Sculptor Henry Moore has been asked not to leave**

any holes in which boys could trap their heads when
he carves "Family Group" for Harlow New Town.'
(News Chronicle)

Presumably girls' heads are expendable! The fairer
sex come in for some criticism from one individual,
writing to the *Daily Telegraph*:

> 'As you pass a group of schoolgirls in the streets
> nowadays, you frequently find them trying to stand
> upside down against a wall – this being one of
> the accomplishments learned in the school hours.
> The whole system of elementary education needs
> overhauling.'

If physical exercise is condemned, then television
advertisements can be, in some cases, recommended.
Writing to the *TV Times*, one viewer says:

> 'I disagree with anyone who says that the
> commercials spoil the programmes, or are a
> waste of time.

> **Some contain useful knowledge. For instance,
> while I was attending a history lesson, a teacher
> asked: "Who was Napoleon Bonaparte's first
> wife?" A boy called out, "Josephine!" "How did
> you know?" asked the teacher. "Well, sir," said the
> boy, "there's a commercial on ITV where Napoleon
> comes in and says: Josephine, look what I've
> brought you!"'**

The entertainment business certainly brings advancement, as can be seen from the case of Mr Mark Brown, whose progress was reported in the *Nairobi Times*; and . . .

> **'. . . who is to appear as a page in the Donovan
> Maule Theatre's revival of *Antigone*. His last
> appearance was in Hillcrest School's production of
> *Alice in Wonderland*, when he played the part of a
> hedgehog.'**

Musicians are often spotted at an early age.

> **It has been known for a fond mother to confess
> that she knew her child would be musical when she
> saw him playing on the linoleum as a baby. The
> sarcastic father has retorted that he considered
> his son had Van Gogh's ear for music, and only
> became convinced of his potential when, on hearing
> a beautiful young girl singing in the shower, the son
> put his ear and not his eye to the keyhole.**

It is one thing for a parent to be sarcastic, but reports have not been confirmed whether the Chairman of Governors, introducing a musical evening, survived this attempted witticism:

> Tonight at this school, the orchestra has promised
> to play like it has never played before – together.

On the subject of pupils and music, the story is
told of the little boy who, after the Christmas Carol
Concert and his class's rendering of *Gloria in Excelsis*,
approached his teacher and asked:

> 'Miss, I know who Joseph is, and I know who Mary
> is – but who is this "Gloria"?'

Speaking of little boys, a dinner lady was giving out
dinner tickets at an Infants' School in Hartlepool:

> 'Are you free?' she asked the little lad.
> 'No, I'm four!' he replied.
> 'No,' she said. 'What I mean is . . . do you have free
> dinners?'
> 'No!' he frowned. 'I only have one!'

and . . .

> Peter went on a Primary School field trip to a
> nature reserve. He told his Mam that when Wayne
> needed to 'spend a penny', he did so among the
> nettles, in front of everybody – AND he got stung.
> 'What did your teacher do?' she asked.
> 'Gave him a dock leaf,' was Peter's reply.

Little girls also have their moments . . .

> Sarah, from Barnstaple, at the age of four and a
> half loved nothing better than to work with the

builders who were working on her parents' kitchen
extension. After nursery on Friday, her Mam went
to collect her, and was passing the time of day with
her teacher. Her Mam told her how Sarah had been
a big help to the builders.

'And will you be helping them next week?' asked
the teacher.

'The boss says it depends whether those b——
bricks arrive!' she replied.

It is easy for young children to make a simple mistake,
as the following examples will bear out:

At the start of the year the Spanish teacher asked
if there had been anyone who had visited Spain
for their holidays. A small boy said he had been to
'San Joo-an' and 'San Jo-zay'. The teacher pointed
out that, in Spanish, the 'J' was not pronounced as
in English, so it should be 'San Hoo-an' and 'San
Ho-zay'.

He asked, 'Now, when did you go?'

'Last Hoon and Hoo-ly, Sir!'

The innocence of children can lead to some unfortunate misunderstandings.

The Catholic Junior School was taken over to
the Parish Church of Our Lady Seat of Wisdom
for the feast of St Peter and St Paul. Before
the service began, Father Butters announced:
'Following our last School Mass here on the Feast
of the Ascension, I should tell you that the bowls
which are placed at the back of the Church and
are labelled "FOR THE SICK" are for donations of
money only.'

If it is easy for children to make simple mistakes, it can be equally as easy for harassed teachers:

> The teacher asked the class who would like to do a turn making farmyard impressions at the Christmas show. Five little children put their hands up and four were chosen – all except for Tony, who could not be trusted. On the night of the show, only two of the children materialized and the teacher was forced to resort to Tony who, sitting in the front row, was only too ready to be of assistance. When it came to his turn, he stood on the stage and, when asked to proceed with his farmyard impression, grabbed the microphone and shouted:
>
> 'For God's sake, will you get off that b——— tractor.'

It is comforting to know that, at the very top of society,

there is a monarch who not only is blessed with all the qualities necessary for her position, but has brains and qualifications in abundance:

> 'Queen Elizabeth, who has a natural equipment of dignity, friendliness and charm of manner, is a great reader, and keeps well abreast of what is happening in the literary world. Her taste is for biography and travel, rather than for fiction. But this, perhaps, is natural, since she has, as a very small girl at school, won prizes for literature and essay writing; and at the age of fourteen she passed the Junior Oxford examination. Hence, it is only appropriate that she should be an Hon. DCL of Oxford, and an Hon. LLD of the Universities of Belfast, Glasgow and St Andrews.'

> *(Landmark)*

It is also reassuring to know that when it came to Prince Charles's education, he was treated no differently from any East End lad – except in minor matters:

> 'Tories as well as socialists should question the wisdom of granting to the three-year-old Prince Charles an income of £10,000 a year. It is never good for a young boy to have too much money to spend.'

> *(Daily Express)*

. . . and, as the *Daily Sketch* informs us:

> 'Prince Charles, aged 18, passed his driving test first bash yesterday. He went through the 45-minute exam at Isleworth, Middlesex, in a special car with

> a special examiner over a special route. Apart from
> that it was quite normal.'
>
> *(Daily Sketch)*

Clearly public school education can have its drawbacks
– many chums, but of the same sex! So what is to be
done when the 'disco-ing' has to start? The *Sunday
Express* has the answer:

> 'After a boarding-school education 18-year-old
> Prince Charles had no difficulty selecting his male
> party guests. But the organizers were forced to
> fall back on *Burke's Peerage* to raise most of the 75
> girl guests.'
>
> *(Sunday Express)*

Such establishments certainly aim at making pupils
'manly', as this report in the *Daily Telegraph* shows.
Unfortunately, being 'manly' these days is not enough:

> 'I have one hope. The young Prince is attending a
> school whose theme is manliness. I say it would
> take a man to get up and say: "No, father, I am
> not coming out with you murdering animals. I am
> going to send a subscription to the League Against
> Cruel Sports instead."'

At the end of the day, it is nice to know that our
children can, of course, behave decorously.

> 'Bristol children are to be shown how to cheer and
> yet remain dignified when Princess Margaret visits
> the city next month.'
>
> *(Daily Mail)*

8
Schools are Like That

There is an unpredictability about working in a school which makes life very interesting. This is inevitable in a community where many individuals are working in close proximity, and where institutions have their own customs and personalities. Because it is people who cause problems, there are always plenty of them, but they also create humour which can come quite unexpectedly, and in many forms.

To ease the running of an institution, it is reasonable to suppose that clear, concise notices distributed in various locations facilitate good order – that is, if they *are* clear. This one was observed by a clergyman attending a retreat at Downside Abbey, and was pinned on a door leading from the boys' school:

NO EXIT FOR BOYS
EXCEPT FOR DISPOSAL OR
RUBBISH

Gastronomically speaking, from a cake sale in the food technology department of a Durham school:

CAKES 66p
UPSIDE-DOWN CAKES 99p

A notice from a Manchester paper is similarly open to misinterpretation:

'B - - - - - School. Wanted in January – Experienced man to take entire responsibility for the lowest form of boys.'

There would seem to be the possibility of recruiting in that case, but surely it is a bit much to expect to obtain someone suitable for this post:

SURREY EDUCATION COMMITTEE

Portley House School,
Whyteleafe Road, Caterham

Qualified TEACHER of the Dead
required at this school

If anyone has experience to fill the following vacancy, advertised in the *Camberley News & Mail*, then *GREEEEE . . . !*

ROYAL GRAMMAR SCHOOL
GUILDFORD
(700 boys 11–18)

Required in January 1984
A PART-TIME
TEACHER OF
MAOOOOOOOO

Approximately 3½ days per week

Did they really want the following type of teacher . . . ?

**SHEFFIELD
BIRKDALE SCHOOL
Full time Teacher of
MATHEMATICS with games
(particularly rugby football)
to teach for GCE 'O' levels**

**Birkdale is an independent
day school, and the applicant
should be a convicted Christian**

It is so important that accurate wording is used – not the case at an English Language School for foreigners in Oxford which, in the dining room, makes this request of students:

'**After your meal, please return your used food.**'

Well, you can make excuses for that, but what about this?

**HARROW SCHOOL CHAPEL
NOT TO BE TAKEN AWAY**

Is someone having a go at the boss in this notice, seen on a staff room notice board in a school in the North-East?

'**If you think you've got a problem, you should see the Head.**'

This stern warning from a Norfolk School loses its impact, thanks to the wrong choice of word:

> 'Will the individual who borrowed a ladder from
> the caretaker last month kindly return same
> immediately, otherwise further steps will be taken.'

The following snippet from the *Lillydale and Yarra Valley Express* conjures up a remarkable picture:

> 'The school is presently sited on about five acres of
> steep land, and has 445 children on the roll.'

From time to time a complete misprint does conjure up a delightful scenario, like this one from the *Merseymart*:

> 'FOR SALE: One large Headmaster answers to the
> name of Jock; house trained £10 or near offer.'

The omission of a minor prefix can make a major difference:

> 'Sir Roger Manwood's Grammar School, Sandwich,
> founded in 1563, will go educational in September
> next year.'
>
> **(Kent Messenger)**

The omission of a single letter could be a case for the Old Age Pensioners' Protection Society. The *Trent and Harrow Recorder* carried this story:

> ### FAMINE
>
> Pupils from Earlsmead First and Middle Schools in
> South Harrow have collected seven sacks of grans
> for famine victims in Africa.

The inclusion of a wrong letter can be embarrassing:

> **'Anti-grammer**
> **battlers**
> **lose fight**
>
> **The Department of Education and Science has at**
> **last approved Bexley Council's proposal to separate**
> **Erith School into two schools . . .'**

Sometimes accurate reporting can cause a shade of red to rise. This item in the *Evesham Journal* must have caused the odd sharp intake of breath:

> **'In all three cases the thieves got in by forcing**
> **open a rear door. They took £15 from Cropthorne**
> **School, £145 from Fladbury and £95.40 of spirits,**
> **cigarettes and cigars from Besford Court, a**
> **special school.'**

It prompts the story of a notice which appeared on a staff room notice board in the Midlands:

**DO YOU HAVE A DRINK PROBLEM?
IF SO, THEN RING WORCESTER 462073**

When the Deputy Head did so out of curiosity, he
found out it was the local off licence!

Some schools don't have the money to buy drink but
there is a wealth of initiative which goes into raising
income. *The Times* reported one such enterprise:

> **'The increasing time spent by schools on activities
> to raise funds for essential educational items was
> deplored by a teachers' conference yesterday. One
> school was said to be running a greyhound at a local
> track to help to buy textbooks.'**

On the subject of betting, this story is told from a
Headteachers' Conference in Harrogate run by a Local
Education Authority. It was the Spring Term, and it
was Grand National Day. A chief adviser attempted
to lighten the Saturday gloom as he was about to
set off on some riveting aspect of inspections. He
turned to one Head, notorious for his love of the
turf, and asked:

> **'Come on, Noel, you're a betting man. Give
> us a tip!'**
> **Without so much as a pause, he looked up and said:**
> **'Don't smoke in bed.'**

Someone who might have been good for a tip but
instead overwhelmed a school in Derbyshire with
his generosity was Mr Lester Piggott, the millionaire
jockey . . .

'. . . who donated one of his old socks to a fund
whose object is the acquistion of a mini-bus for a
comprehensive school in Derbyshire.'

The need to raise funds often means that schools have
to court local businesses. At an institution in the north
of England, local magnates were invited to a pleasant
luncheon to inaugurate a business initiative. A large
number turned up for the food and wine, which
prompted the Headteacher to tell this story:

'I am reminded, looking at such a large
representation from local commerce, of a tale
told to me by one of my Jewish friends. Isaac
was on his death bed, and was surrounded by
his family. He half-opened his eyes and asked in a
whisper:
"Are you there, Rebecca?"
"I am, my husband," she replied.
"Are you there, Jacob?"
"I am, my Father," he replied.
"Are you there, Jessica?"
"I am, my Father," she replied.
"Then who the hell is looking after the shop?"
he asked.'

The Headteacher of St Michael's Roman Catholic
School once received a phone call from the local
Sixth Form College, asking him if he would be
prepared to give a talk to a group on the retail
trade. He replied that, much as he would like to, he
knew very little about it, and enquired why it was
that he had been contacted. The secretary on the
line explained that she had been given a list by the
Careers teacher, and asked to fix up talks. Opposite

the Headteacher's name had appeared the words:
'St Michael's'.
   'You DO work for Marks and Spencer?' she
genuinely asked.

In this age of local management of schools, funding
depends more on the numbers of pupils than any
external revenue which can be raised. It comes, then, as
no surprise to read this item in the *Daily Telegraph*:

> 'The Revd Glyn Wilkinson, the Rector of Barwick,
> near Leeds, has told his parishioners to produce
> more babies so that the village infant school can
> be saved.'

It is surprising how only a slight rise in numbers can
cause difficulties. The *Western Mail* gives this piece of
information:

> 'Griffiths town Junior School was designed to
> take 420 pupils. It now has 421, and is seriously
> overcrowded.'

Better too many than too few! Sometimes closure can
come from the most unexpected areas. The *Montreal
Gazette* reported the end of this institution:

> 'The privately owned Harbinger School of Business
> shut down yesterday because of financial problems.'

To be freed from the threat of penury, schools must
establish and maintain a reputation for success which
is accepted in the locality, so that parents want to send
their children there. The *Brentford and Chiswick Times*

reports on a Head who feels his school is achieving satisfactory levels:

> 'He said that the school had managed to maintain a good standard. Few boys left the school unable to read or write. "In this age of television," he said, "this is no mean achievement."'

But should not the Head of the following establishment hold up his hands in shame and horror at the failure of his pupils . . . ?

> 'I was horrified to hear a young woman, a product of our primary schools, where I presume history and geography are taught, ask: "Where is Poona?" Can nothing be done to teach young people about the historic greatness of the Empire and of important places in it?'

Others who do not seek academic excellence strive unsuccessfully to master even the basics of their chosen profession. A Welsh newspaper carried this report:

> 'A solicitor told Falmouth Magistrates that Richard Archibald Jerum Clark, of Penrhyn, was not cut out to be a criminal. When he committed a burglary at Penrhyn Infants' School with two inexperienced thieves, they wore proper gloves. He had on a pair of the fingerless variety, said Mr Timothy Goldburn.'

When such individuals are caught the fate they suffer might be bad, but it could have been much worse, as the *Star* suggests:

> 'Ordering the boy to be sent to an approved school

for three years, the Chairman, Col. F. G. Barker,
said: "What a dreadful commentary on modern
education and religion. If he were at Eton, he would
be flogged out of his life."'

Perhaps he should have found a suitable course
for 'breaking and entering'. It would appear that
courses for most things are available, as this advert
in the *Manchester Association of University Teachers'
Newsletter* would serve to demonstrate:

> 'Sexual Harassment Training School. Wednesday
> 6 May at AUT Head Office. Does anyone want
> to participate? All expenses paid, including child
> care costs.'

At the end of the day what it is all about is that
inspirational education encapsulated in this news item
from the *Salisbury Journal*:

> 'As Hannibal urged his 40,000 men and 37 elephants
> across the Alps in 218 BC, he could have had little
> idea that he would be followed 2,200 years later by
> a party of 20 boys and four masters from Oswestry
> School, among them 14-year-old Stephen Jones,
> from Bulford Camp.'

Well, strike me down with an ivory tusk!

9

Learning

The 'quality of learning' is something very much in the minds of inspectors who nowadays are as welcome in schools as a burst boiler in January. The elegant, unaggressive style of Her Majesty's Inspectors of yore is in marked contrast to the perceived Rottweilerish tendencies of the modern hit squads of registered inspectors and their assistants.

The present love/hate relationship between these people and schools is well-expressed in this witticism from an education journal:

The scene is two teachers reading a gravestone upon which is written:

R.I.P
F.M. STURD

A
GENTLEMAN
AND A
SCHOOLS
INSPECTOR

One teacher says to the other:
'I wonder what the name of the inspector was.'

The grim humour directed at OFSTED has become more vitriolic as they progress through the schools of this country, spreading unacceptable pressures and providing little value for money – a resentment reflected in the following:

Question: What is the difference between an OFSTED Inspector and a terrorist?
Answer: You can negotiate with a terrorist.

A plane crashed on the North York Moors, and there were three survivors – a teacher, a caretaker and an OFSTED inspector. They eventually arrived, late at night, at an isolated smallholding, where the farmer gave them food but informed them that he had only two beds to spare, so that one of them would have to sleep in the barn. The caretaker volunteered, but after a few minutes there was a knock on the door. It was the caretaker, who said: 'I'm sorry, but I won't be able to sleep in the barn. I didn't realize there were two cats there, and I suffer from asthma.'

'It's OK – I'll go,' said the teacher.

Two minutes later, there was a knock at the door, and this time it was the teacher, who said: 'I'm sorry, but I can't sleep in the barn – there are two pigs in there, and whenever I'm near them I get a severe migraine.'

'I'll go,' said the OFSTED Inspector.

A few minutes later, there was yet another knock on the door. When it was opened – the two pigs and two cats were standing there!

Then there was the OFSTED inspector who was prosecuted for assaulting a tortoise. When asked the reason for his aggression, he replied:

'It had been following me around all day!'

The intense and unreasonable pressure imposed by these inspectors, particularly and paradoxically, upon the most conscientious teachers, is reflected humorously (or perhaps hysterically) in the following tale:

A little boy of six pulled on the coat tail of the OFSTED inspector as he sauntered around the class. He asked the inspector if he was Jesus.

'No, no, I'm not, my boy,' the inspector replied.

Shortly afterwards, the little lad was back.

'Are you sure you're not Jesus?'

'Yes, I'm sure. I'm not Jesus.'

Ten minutes later, the child reappeared. 'Are you really, really sure you are not Jesus?'

'I am really, really sure I am not Jesus. Why do you keep asking me, for Heaven's sake?'

'Because when you came up the path, Miss was

looking out of the window, and she said: "Oh, Jesus
– here he comes!"'

Schools which are perceived to be inadequate, or
'failing', having undergone OFSTED, are not spared
public wrath and condemnation. Rarely do we hear
of the mindless 'cock-ups' of inspectors who, in some
cases, have done for education what Vinny Jones has
done for finesse and fair play in soccer. To help put
the record slightly to rights, we learn that:

> **'OFSTED, the government' education watchdog,
> made up of fair-minded, independent worthies, has
> been inspecting schools in Kent.**
>
> One primary school in Sittingbourne received a
> particularly damning report. The inspectors were
> most critical of teaching standards there, pointing
> to a certain class of children they had observed who
> had failed to learn anything of significance since
> they had been at the school.
>
> They found the class showed no evidence of
> even being able to read, write or add up. It later
> emerged that the class was made up of four and
> five-year olds who had been in school for a total of
> ten days.'

Returning to happier times, teachers from a school in
Hartlepool remember with affection meeting, in a local
pub, an HMI who had just completed an inspection
in their school. As he sniffed snuff from an ivory-bore
tusk, he entertained them with examples of toilet
graffiti he had collected throughout his educational
journeys. His favourites:

> **'My mother made me a homosexual.'**

Underneath was written . . .

'If I give her the wool, will she make me one?'

. . . and at an English school in Cairo:

'We have Pharaohs at the bottom of our garden.'

This heading from the *Nursery World* is indicative of the learning problems facing a number of pupils – not to mention the reporter . . .

WHAT IS DYSELXIA?

In cases of learning difficulties, it is useful for teachers, parents and pupils to have quite specific advice on how to improve and where to find help. *What's On In and Around Faringdon* makes the basic mistake of assuming too much:

'CAN YOU READ? IF NOT, PHONE 21167.'

Sometimes pupils seem prepared to accept abuse from bullying teachers and then commend them unto death in their quest for effective learning.

This is one sentiment expressed in the *Old Kimboltian Newsletter*:

> 'I was a dunce at mathematics and Banty Gibbard used a sort of refined torture on me. He leaned over me as I was attempting some problems in algebra, and if I was getting it wrong, he fixed the two ends of the clasp of his key ring on the lobe of my ear and increased pressure until I cried out in pain. At his funeral, there were no family mourners, but a full Church paid tribute to an unselfish and kindly man.'

It is not, of course, always the pupil who has the learning difficulty. A parent, writing to the letters page of the *Sunday Express*, maintains:

> 'My little girl wrote: "The farmer said: 'Let's start now.'" Her teacher altered this to: "The farmer suggested that we commenced at once."'

Such obsession with complexity does nothing for learning. As a post-script however, it must be added that the teacher in question has since got a job writing OFSTED Reports.

Meanwhile, it would appear from *The Times of India*, that the way to a man's brain is through his stomach. Or could it be that there is some aspect of the use of technology in education we have yet to come across?

> **'We assure fluency in English in two months. British School of Language staff trained by foreign mission. Method: Microwave.'**

Having mastered the language, clear, pithy explanations in a diagrammatic and visual form, no matter how simple, are always welcome in the learning process. Well, that is if your pride permits it. An item from the *Bookseller* says much about the technological revolution within our armed services and the importance of their street credibility:

> **'It was a week of surprises for Ladybird Books. First of all, the Ministry of Defence asked them for a set of books on how computers work; since, however, the Ladybirds on this subject are designed for 9 to 15-year-olds, the military, with a proper regard for camouflage, asked that their brass should be enabled to read these concise introductions behind plain covers. Ladybird declined this request.'**

Motivation and enjoyment are helpful ingredients in encouraging learning, but sometimes the efforts of some to better themselves are high-handedly thwarted. The *Daily Telegraph* carried this confession:

> **'But it certainly was not the picture the whole time I was there,' Dr Terence Lawlor told an inquiry into conditions at the Normansfield Hospital, Teddington, Middlesex. He agreed that patients so lacked stimulation that one morning they were seen watching a television test card. Another morning Dr Lawlor said he found them watching an Open University programme on Einstein's Theory of Relativity. "I changed it to a cartoon," he added.'**

Sometimes accuracy of texts is sacrificed for the best, or worst, of motives. The *Scottish Community Drama Association Bulletin* carried this piece of censorship news:

> '**A school edition of Hamlet in use in the Midlands of England, changes Shakespeare's "Enter a bloody sergeant" to "Enter a bleeding captain".**'

... and from a *Cambridge University Newsletter*:

> '**We apologize for the fact that in the title of a recent talk in the last newsletter, the words "theoretical physics" came out as "impossible ideas".**'

This would seem about right to a headmaster of Rugby School who told the assembled school on Speech Day about an advertisement in the *Careers Organization Bulletin*, which read:

> '**WANTED: Man to work on nuclear fissionable isotope molecular reactive counters and three-phase cyclotronic uranium photosynthesizers. No experience necessary.**'

Amazing information can come to light in the search for knowledge. The *East Kent Mercury* must have set the literary world alight with this revelation:

> '**Walmer Social and Educational Centre used the theme drama selections with members portraying characters from *Romeo & Juliet*, *Anthony and Cleopatra* and *Worzel Gummidge* (one of Shakespeare's more obscure plays).**'

And how will Dads feel about this shattering piece of research from *The Times*?

> **'Mr Scotland referred to the children's knowledge of current affairs and its expression in terms of hero worship, which, he said, placed Sir Winston Churchill first, followed by "mother", Mr Elvis Presley and the Pope.'**

The Times does indeed seem to have the finger on the pulse of the common man, as can further be seen from this item which should go down a bundle on the inner-urban estates of our great cities:

> **'The company's book, *Sellocraft*, is a little mine of items that children can make for themselves and for each other, using normal household objects (like champagne corks).'**

The Reverend Dr John Quillan, quoted in the *Glasgow Evening Times*, has managed to come up with a new interpretation of Gibbons' *Decline and Fall* which is so obvious. He said that it was with horror that he looked on the very thought of sex education in schools.

> **'Sex education,' he declared, 'resulted in the fall of the Roman Empire.'**

Talking about foreigners, did you also know that the Newcastle and Gateshead Water Co. is now managed from Lyons in France?

> **'In ICI Wilton there is a gateman who can express instructions to foreign lorry drivers in about ten languages. In any one language his vocabulary is**

**no more than thirty key words. The company has
developed a system for him and taught him the
linguistic basics for the job,' said Mr Hagen.**

At least physicist Stefan Marinor, writing in *New
Scientist,* believes the pupils in our schools have
acquired basic skills:

> **'Any child can immediately calculate by using
> formula (1) (E mot = v.rot A) that for v = V = 300
> km/s, I = 100A, b = 14.8cm, bo = 0.2cm (so that
> In(2b/bo) = In I 48 = 5) the induced tension will
> be 60V.'**

But at the end of the day, forget about the 'quality
of learning and teaching', because we all can rely
upon our pupils completing their homework which,
according to the *TES:*

> **'. . . may have, however, a distant ring: what
> perhaps should be considered is the provision
> of standardized learning opportunities outside
> the teacher-directed environment towards the
> development of learning skills and the achievement
> of some degree of educational self-sufficiency.'**

So . . . now we know!

10
Advertisements

A look at adverts for posts in educational establishments often brings to light misspellings, or a description or a turn of phrase which speaks volumes. At times, the slip is eminently reasonable, and perhaps is an unconscious expression of the writer's state of mind. This one, from the *Horticultural Week*, seems to demand skills way beyond those which can be reasonably expected:

> **Head gardener required. This residential school for students with learning difficulties requires an experienced full-time gardener with responsibility for the maintenance of staff and students. Apply to St Joseph's School, Amlets Lane, Cranleigh, Surrey.**

If that seems unreasonable, how about this one from the *Nairobi Standard*:

> **Situation Vacant. Teacher. Wanted teacher of English for a leading secretarial college, part-time. English speaking an advantage, excellent prospects.**

And from the *Carmarthen Journal*:

Part-Time School Receptionist

Applicants should have some knowledge of
clerical work and the ability to speak would be an
advantage.

On the other hand, what is really important in West
Glamorgan is that you can speak the vernacular:

Head of FRENCH Department to teach the subject
to GCE 'A' level. The subject is taught entirely
in Welsh.

(County Job Bulletin)

It would appear from the following two adverts in *The
Teacher* that whoever penned them must have had an
eye on his retirement, and had just returned from a
traumatic afternoon at the local baths:

**NORTHWOOD PREPARATORY SCHOOL
(MOOR PARK)**
require as soon as possible a
LUNCHTIME PLAY SUPERVISOR
for our 408 year old boys.
Please tel. Mrs Hampel on
Northwood (09274) 25648

And . . .

Assistant Teacher (Scale I) required
for September to teach
an Infant/Junior class.
Applications are invited from persons
who have an interest in swimming.

Sometimes the desperation to obtain a body to put in

front of a class is such that it does not really matter whether or not that someone is suitable:

BLADON HOUSE SCHOOL

**Residential maladjusted HOUSEMASTER
required as soon as possible.**

(Burton Daily Mail)

A new slant on the all-consuming world of pedagogy comes from the programme of a one-day course for professional tutors of newly-qualified teachers in East Sussex:

Teaching as an educational activity, 4.45–5.00

We can only applaud one of the courses offered during the Autumn Term by the *Institute of Education, University of London*, for providing the very real opportunity for 'hands-on (*or heads-off*) experience':

**Empathy and rôle play in the teaching of history;
6 and 7 December 1989. (Day 2 will be held at the
Tower of London.)**

Doubtless governors, heads and parents will flock to contact the organizer of a one-day conference presented by the *British Society for Research on Sex Education*, who advertise:

**Sex Education: Who's responsible? Please write for
further details to ROSE.**

So it was Rose all the time . . . !

It has often been said that the most important

person in the school is the caretaker. From time to time, as a report in the *Nottingham Post* shows, they can add extra stress to the lives of students:

> **Mr Alan Black of the Nottingham Health Authority has had to apologize to the ten people who attended his first 'Why Worry?' an anti-anxiety course after the caretaker of the school in which they were meeting locked them in for the night.**

At other times the job itself is just reward for taking the time to bother sending in an application to the correct address:

> **TURKEY
> VACANCY**
>
> **For the teachers of English with teaching cert. high salary, acc., return ticket.**
>
> **Apply to (Ozel Kocaeli Lisesi CUKURBAG MAL. Mantarcesme sok. Portaka Hafiz Konagi No. 82 Izmit/Kocaeli/Turkey) inc. recent photo and CV.**

After all of that, if you are still desperate for a job, why not present exemplary credentials prepared by S. Denner, who advertised in the *Worthing & District Advertiser*:

> **A awful CV can loose you that job. we do the best – call Worthing 212280. Typing Express**

Adverts for education courses abound, and often reveal a hitherto hidden perception on the part of the organizers. This one, from an announcement of a two-day conference on artificial intelligence held by *Social and Educational Applications of Knowledge Engineering Centre* at Brighton Polytechnic, carries with it an interesting social perception of the teaching profession:

Normal fee £45; Teachers, community workers, students and unwaged £10 per day.

11
Parents

Parents can always be relied upon to support strong discipline in schools. When the harsh system of punishments is described at New Intake Parents' Meetings, they nod in agreement at detention, beam with acquiescence at exclusion, and if knee-capping and decapitation were part of the menu, they would positively swoon with ecstasy – that is, if it applies to other people's offspring.

From time to time the child is innocent, and it is the parent who is culpable. A report in the *Birmingham Post* carried the following story:

> **'The mother complained that her son, an only child, was becoming truculent, had started smoking, had been seen entering a public house, and was keeping company with a girl. Inspector McCann began to investigate. "I found that the son was 36!" he said.'**

Parents may also complain that their progeny are the butt of jokes which are causing them upset and never think that they should have considered whether it was wise to have called him 'Zap', 'Algernon' or 'Clint'. All very acceptable names, indeed, but ones which don't always go down well on estates where Rottweiler dogs seek cover. The test of an acceptable name is when, as a parent, you are able to shout through an open window into a street crowded with children playing football, or who are just standing around, crunching the odd empty can, to inform X his tea is ready. If 'Claude', 'Aloysius' or 'Cardew' does not bring a wide-eyed hush and nudges in the back alley, then go for it! But take care, for the same fate might befall you as it did this mother mentioned among the letters in the *Daily Herald*:

> 'I knew a woman who named her son "Gabriel", but she always called him "Sidney". It was not until he left school that he discovered his real name. He was so embarrassed by it that he refused to show his birth certificate to anyone, refused to work, and drifted into a life of crime.'

Commiserations, then, to the following, and shame to their parents:

> 'Russell Sprout', 'Cockshott Smith', 'Jock Strap', 'Rose Plant', 'Isabel Donger', 'A. Pratt' and 'V.D. Jones'.

Ambition is a wonderful motivator and is often stronger in parents for their children than in the children themselves. This can, of course, lead to great problems when the child does not share the parent's ambition. *The Times* reported:

> 'Corporation bus crews in Nottingham could not understand why the same violin was left on buses once a fortnight for two months and had to be claimed at the Lost Property Office. An official explained yesterday that it belonged to a little girl who did not want to go to music lessons. After paying the lost property charge for the fourth time, her father said: "She will learn the violin even if it kills me!".'

From time to time a parent's ambitions are realized and the determination to publicize an offspring's achievements can manifest itself in the most strange and indeed desperate situations.

One is reminded of the fond and over-protective mother who, sitting on the beach at Whitley Bay, noticed her grown-up son was having difficulties on his surf-board. She rushed towards the lifeguard shouting:

> 'My son, the doctor, is drowning.'

A dubious ambition is expressed by a parent writing to the *Daily Mirror*:

> 'How can I get my two-year-old daughter interested in television? We sit her in front of the set. She watches for a minute, and says: "Switch off, Mummy!" I should hate to think that my daughter will grow up uninterested in TV!'

Television, indeed, figures largely in the psyche of parents. While some curse them for their insipid distractions which lure their children from homework, sport, normal conversation and the healthy life, others clearly embrace them as the panaceas of all ills.

The *Brighton Evening Argos* carried the story of the father of a nine-year-old boy brought before Brighton Juvenile Court for stealing an ignition key from a car, who said:

> **'We have tried to do everything for him. I have just installed a television set for him. We cannot do any more.'**

If only behaviour moderation were so easy . . . Wait – it would appear that the mystical qualities of the power of the box might not be as far-fetched as cynics would have us believe. A parent writing to the *Daily Mirror* presents the case:

> **'Three of my children went to approved schools for minor offences. Another was beginning to go**

> the same way until I got a TV on the HP. The
> boy became as good as gold. He started to go to
> Church after watching services on television, and
> would not go out even when we wanted him to.
> Since the set went back because of non-payments,
> he has reverted to his old ways.'

At least one parent has attempted to claim TV viewing
as a measure of MENSA status:

> 'My daughter, aged nearly three, can switch the
> television on by herself. Is this a record?'
> (Letter in *Brighton Evening Argos*)

When the television is turned on these days, goodness
gracious, obscene utterances might be heard, warns the
Daily Herald:

> 'How careful one must be when a TV camera
> or mike lurks nearby. In *News Review* (BBC 2.35)
> Princess Margaret shouted: "What?" to an official
> she didn't quite hear.
> 'The parents I spoke to afterwards were
> unanimous. They all teach their children to say
> "Pardon?"'

Physical punishment might be anathema in schools,
but many parents are still convinced of its efficacy in
the strangest of forms. *Reveille* reported the case of a
mother who was convinced of her tactics:

> 'She had two teenage children who, when younger,
> went through a phase of biting people. "I bit them
> back and they stopped. My son, when about five,
> threw his dinner on the floor. I tipped a plate of

custard over him. He has never thrown any food about since."'

The mind boggles to think what she might have done had either of them failed to reach the toilet in time . . .

A report appeared in the *Sunday Mirror*, concerning a mother when she slapped her little boy hard after he had demolished a display of canned foods in the supermarket. Facing the hostile stares of assistants, the mother said in a loud voice:

> **'If I don't correct him now, he might grow up to be a student.'**

Instead he grew up to be a Mafia hit-man!

Children can at times be more than a little provocative, and it is a tribute to the teaching profession that the vast majority have the strength of character not to throttle the odd classful. Even some members of the public whose ways of life are dedicated to a pacific philosophy can lose control.

> The *Peebles Gazette* carried the story of one man who was arrested in the street as he was about to cuff a particularly obnoxious boy:
> 'Mr John Deedow, an organic herb farmer, explained that, in fact, he was rehearsing the part of Othello, "a rôle that demands extravagant gestures". This explanation was sent on a postcard because Mr Deedow and his girlfriend were "attending a festival of peace".'

Parents, usually, are very decent individuals who are prepared to go to any lengths to provide for their children. In the odd case, however, you do get a situation where the parent expects the child to make the provision. The comments of a wife speaking at a North Kent Court and reported in the *Evening News* indicate just how low some Dads are prepared to sink:

> 'My husband cut himself so severely in forcing open the children's moneybox that he had to spend the contents on lint and bandages.'

But if you are not satisfied with the children you have, then why not try and think of a way of making a substitution, like the father in the *News Chronicle*:

> 'The probation officer said that at one time the father told him that he had thought of having all his

> children looked after by relatives, so that he could
> devote more time to unwanted children.'

Thankfully married couples wish, generally, to retain
their offspring, and if they decide not to have any, then
often there is a very good reason for not doing so. The
Los Angeles Times carried this story:

> 'Dennis Shamblin, 102, who recently applied for a
> marriage licence to marry Marie Gibson, 60, says he
> does not plan to have children. "My eyes are giving
> me trouble!" he explained.'

If he thinks his sight holds the secret to his procreative
talents, it would seem as though his memory is not all
it was . . .

Not all parents are crusading in their efforts to
ensure that their children make the most of their
abilities. Apocryphal they may be, but sometimes one
can recognize the situation:

> 'Dad, can I go to school like the other lads?'
>   'Shut up, Walter, and keep dealing!'

> 'Dad, Can I have an encyclopaedia?'
>   'No, you can go to school on your bike like the
> other kids!'

However, other parents are determined that their
children will succeed whatever the cost, and do not
take kindly to a lack of success:

> Interviewed in the washroom of Tomlinson Junior
> High School, Dean William Stansfield, the Head of
> the school's music faculty, said: 'I was conducting

the graduation ceremony, when a figure dressed
as Tickles the Clown, who was carrying a string
of balloons and singing a song called *Hayrick Soup*,
came on stage and smashed a large cheesecake into
my face. When I had wrestled him to the boards,
several children identified him as Mr James Dorio,
the father of Mary Dorio, a pupil I had been obliged
to "fail".'

Failure or success depends, of course, as much upon
the quality of the school as upon the encourage-
ment of parents. It is, then, pleasing to hear when
parental preferences have been accepted ... well,
more or less.

Overheard on a bus in Gateshead ...
   '... Which big school is your granddaughter going
to go to now that she's 11?'
   'Oh, they've decided to send her to the local
Testicle College.'

A common complaint among parents is that things 'ain't wot they used to be'. Nothing is more designed to alienate children than the words, 'When I was a ...' or 'You would never have got away with that in my day!' Typical of such painful reminiscences is this item which appeared in the *Reynolds News*:

> **'My father made me come home at 10 p.m until I was 21, took my £3 wages, and gave me ten shillings to spend. My own son smokes fairly heavily at 18, earns £120 a week, has several girlfriends and talks of buying a car. Other parents tell me their children seem very grown-up. Could it be something to do with the nuclear bomb tests?'**

Well, there is that possibility, but the likelihood is his father was a miserable and greedy old so-and-so!

Still, misjudgements and being out of touch with reality are relatively common, as can be clearly seen in this letter to the *Daily Express*:

> **'I come of good, working-class stock, but, through always working for and with gentlefolk of England, have always voted Tory, believing that, through their educational advantages, they have the brains to rule this England of ours wisely and well.'**

It was thus that wealth and refined accents bought power, privilege and destruction.

While on the subject of an élite and the rest, it will be a comfort to the vast majority of us to realize that even the most learned and intellectually privileged parent can act in an irrational, or even silly, fashion. This was the case of the dapper, white bearded Cambridge professor. According to the *News Chronicle*:

> **'He went to the Local Authority for sex education pamphlets for his two sons.**
>   **"But I was so alarmed in case my wife should see them that I had to throw them out."'**

If parents are so irrational, should they ever be allowed near their own – or anybody else's – children?

Arguably, only after the most rigorous and sophisticated training. Such a course was advertised in the *North Carolina Spectator*:

> **'LECTURE ON PARENTING – "Putting Parents in Charge", by martial arts expert, John Lamont.'**

If parents can't win 'em all, then at least they can go down fighting . . .

12

... And Into Further Education

Children are born, go to infant school, primary school, and then secondary school. These are years of great trauma for parents – and for many it's not over yet! Parents these days are often forced to scrimp and save for years in order to put their loved ones through higher education. This frugality is usually based on the twin assumptions that it will be 'all worth it in the end', and that their children will be spending all their time away burning the midnight oil in diligent study. If only the truth were known, parents might simply cut their losses and live it up for a bit – just like their offspring.

What students learn, of course, is enough to tax the greatest brains of the nation. This is proved by a recent report in the *Sunday Telegraph* of a discovery of profound significance for the future of mankind. Apparently:

'Mathematical rules have now been devised to

allow pedestrians to remain as dry as possible when caught in a shower of rain. The calculations were made by Mr M. Scott, a mathematician of Durham University. "When walking into the rain, one should lower the head and walk as fast as possible. When the rain is coming from behind, one should either walk forward leaning backwards, or backwards leaning forward, at a deliberate pace."'

It's strange, isn't it, that the great verities of life are so obvious, when one comes to think of it . . . !

However, we still lag behind America when it comes to major breakthroughs in learning. Unfortunately, some students in the land of opportunity fail to recognize their luck and proceed to make unjustifiable complaints. One Joey Young of California even went so far as to sue the University of California on the spurious grounds that he learned nothing. His case was that:

'Five of us signed up for a course in degree Basketball. The first four lessons were called "The ball and how to throw and catch it". Coach Winner took us through throwing and catching on the blackboard. Finally, when we got to a fieldwork class, the coach admitted that he did not have a ball, and asked if we could supply one. After we dropped out, we were sent tuition bills for $14,000.'

The learned Coach Winner replied: "They said they wanted a meaningful education. That means starting with the basics. I find myself in a situation that is incomparable to prior situations."'

It would be churlish to do anything but sympathize with such a genius.

However, university staff may be clever, but they can still be wrong. Professor Richard Lacey of Leeds University found his knowledge counted for naught recently. A housewife complained about the quality of water in Yeadon, so he tested it and found:

> **'500 live worms and 100 million bacteria in one fluid ounce.'**

Fortunately, the common sense of the layman in the form of Yorkshire Water, then took over. They also tested the water and found it 'perfectly satisfactory', according to a spokesman.

Talking of professors, this graffiti was seen on a wall at Essex University:

> **'Old professors never die. They just lose their faculties.'**

Meanwhile, some universities have devised rules for the correct behaviour to assume in the library – lying prone and gently snoring. This has been encapsulated in a brief report in *The Times* from Cambridge University. A librarian there said:

> **'We welcome sleepers here. A sleeping reader is less of a menace to books than a waking one.'**

Next they'll be claiming that the most popular book is *A Midsummer Night's Dream*!

But college life is not all cramming. There are still some innocent relaxations to be had. Not so long ago, *The Times* reported on the activities of students at a famous redbrick university. It claims that:

> **'About 50 students broke into the college, smashing a pane of glass and chanting: "No cuts! No cuts!" A porter had his hand injured. The police have been informed.'**

Some students, we regret to say, are now so unruly that they fail to pay due regard to their elders and betters. Lady Lewisham once found this to her cost when addressing a group at a college. The *Daily Mirror* of that time noted sombrely that:

> **'The rumpus reached its climax when the good lady (or wretched lady, depending on your point of view) told students: "Often I found that where Socialist**

voters lived, there were dirty milk bottles on the doorstep."'

The joys of riotous behaviour are not, of course, an especially recent phenomenon. Indeed, trying to pretend that students live a virtuous and peaceful life, the *St Andrews University Brochure* claims that:

> **'Apart from an isolated incident of violence in 1470, when the Dean of the Faculty of Arts was shot at with bows and arrows, and, if one glosses over the Jacobite demonstrations of 1715, the university has been singularly free of student unrest.'**

Part of the trouble must lie with the staff these youngsters are forced to mix with.

> **'One Mr John Pawlec, for example, a cook of 14 years' standing at Braesnose College, Oxford, was told by his boss that he was boiling eggs in the wrong way for the "young masters". He promptly went berserk in the kitchen, and destroyed over £1,000 of equipment.'**

Sometimes, of course, trouble at university is so outlandish that, if parents fully realized the depths of depravity, then they would rush to remove their children at once. It is therefore lucky that this report from the *Guardian* has not been more widely publicized:

> **'A spokesman for the university Proctor's office said that no disciplinary action had been taken over skirt lengths, but an examination official said: "We may get some trouble with the English Literature lot next Thursday. They are more temperamental."'**

To some, of course, it is all slightly disappointing, or at least confusing. The *Guardian*, once more, wrote that:

> **'Other students found university life less immoral than they expected, and one girl was pleasantly surprised to find that students are "just ordinary people like myself and, in fact, not all Socialists".'**

Students, indeed, may be totally lascivious and immoral – but they will listen to reason, as a Methodist minister, one Reverend Cyril Downes, once found out. The *Daily Mail* learned that he had:

> **'A heart-to-heart talk with the Sheffield students who are putting on Oscar Wilde's *Salome* on the Festival Fringe next week. Result: When Salome, dark-haired, willowy, 20-year-old Jill Stevens, peels off the last of her seven veils, she will be revealed in – a flared skirt and tunic blouse with sleeves.'**

All these pleasures don't come cheap. 'Strapped for cash' is a saying heard in many a household, in the hope that it will lead to a doting parent forking out yet more hard-earned money. When this plea fails, students have to turn to other ways to get by. Unfortunately, there are not many options open to the young and poor. Thus, according to the *Daily Telegraph*:

> **'Britain's 100,000 undergraduates and students returning from vacation this month will be told not to deal with fellow-students selling shirts, jewellery and other finery to earn extra cash.'**

However, it's not all doom and gloom, because the report concludes: 'But insurance selling at universities will be allowed because it is considered enterprising.'

There is one particular parent who hasn't had to make great financial sacrifices – and neither has her daughter. The *Sun* reports Mrs Thatcher as saying:

'"I can't understand all the fuss about student grants. Carol managed to save out of hers. Of course, we paid for her ski-ing holidays."

"And Mark, of course, never even went to college, which is a pity, for had he studied geography, he might never have got lost in the desert."'

It is, of course, all worth it in the end, because those with a degree are incisive, intelligent and worldly. They know how to act in a crisis. We should all take this lesson on quick-thinking from the *Hartlepool Mail* as proof of the value of such an education:

> **'Smith, a politics student at Grey College, told the Court: "I didn't think they would believe my name was Smith because I had no identification on me, so I told them it was Jones."'**

Student Smith came from the same college as the young man who went on a pub crawl and then took a taxi back to Durham.

> **'The fare was £200. He had unfortunately forgotten that the pub crawl took place in Edinburgh – 150 miles away.'**

Never mind! Students are taught to take any reverse with great good humour. Well, most of them do. The *Daily Telegraph* some time ago carried this apology to a new president of the Oxford Union who had worked as a navvy before going up to Oxford. The apology concluded:

> **'Owing to a mis-hearing on the telephone, it was stated that he was a former Nazi. The mistake is much regretted.'**

13

Public Schools

The popular image of public schools, held by 'The Great Unwashed', is that they are places of privilege inhabited by spoilt, wealthy youngsters with refined accents, who are detached from the realities of life. They are perceived as institutions smiled upon by the Establishment where practices are tolerated which in state schools would be regarded as worthy of prosecution. In these places, sanctified by the previous presence of those such as Churchill and Gordon of Khartoum, and protected by the 'Old Boy' network of Cabinet ministers and judges, bullying appears to be synonymous with character-building, sloshing food in all directions with high spirits and superciliousness with confidence. Ex-pupils progress not because they are particularly talented, but because they have connections and, of course, privilege begets privilege.

The *Hornsea Journal* makes a valid point:

> **'A public school which stressed that it inculcated the Christian virtue of humility would not get anywhere.'**

Public schools do not have to meet the National
Curriculum requirements as do state schools. This is
roughly the equivalent of Arsenal and Chelsea pleasing
themselves whether they keep to the FA rules, or the
Kray Brothers devising a system of law and order for
the East End.

This image is not helped by the renderings of
ex-public school boys who perpetrate this caricature
of pomposity. This letter in *The Times* seems to
encapsulate all that is obnoxious about those who
feel they have been chosen by God:

> **'Sir, The people of Bermuda are to be
> congratulated on the appointment of such an
> able and fair-minded administrator as their new
> Governor. I should know. I was once St Peter
> Ramsbotham's fag at Eton.'**

'And I still have the scars to prove it!' he might have
added. Regarding that story, one wonders whether
a previous generation had, in fact, for reasons of
etiquette, changed the surname from *Ramsbottom*.

> **The story is told of a visitor arriving at Winchester
> School and asking the Secretary for the bursar, Mr
> Sidebottom.
> 'Sidebottom?' re-iterated the Secretary
> quizzically. 'We have no one of that name, but
> we do have a Mr Siddeebottom.' 'That'll be him!'
> said the debt collector. 'Tell him Mr Testicles
> (pronouncing it Testi-clees) would like to see him.'**

There is no doubt that there is a type of masonic support among those who have attended the same public

school, perhaps a result of the common experience of a miserable and depressed youth.

This item in the *News Chronicle* would appear to substantiate the view:

> **'Mutual trust seems to grow more naturally between people who have attended the same school, fagged for and flogged one another.'**

Fagging, which for those of us unfamiliar with this peculiar primitive practice, and which appears to have about as much attraction as having one's head shoved down the toilet (or should we refer to it as the jakes, the Bogs or the Thunderbox) on a daily basis, clearly has its supporters, as can be seen from this letter to *The Times*:

> **'Sir, I read with dismay that the Public Schools Commission advocates, among other things, the abolition of the fagging system. I wonder how many mothers will deplore this, and I remember well the joy in the realization after only one term at public school, that my son could dust, clean shoes, cook himself simple meals, all very expertly, and how useful was the tip that usually arrived the first week of the school holidays.'**

According to ex-hostage John McCarthy, and as reported by the *Hertfordshire Mercury*, it is not only 'fagging' which can provide useful life-skills. John's educational experiences appear to have saved his life:

'His Haileybury schooling, he said, had helped him
survive his primitive cell conditions – for most of
the time he was tied up and blindfolded.'

The qualities bestowed by the educational experiences
of such schools prompt one to ask why Britain does
not rule the world, or have a healthy economy, and
why England did not qualify for the 1994 World Cup.
Certainly the judge in this case reported in the *East
Anglian Daily Times* credits such institutions with great
influence:

'Anthony John Summers, 17, who was expelled from
an Essex public school for smoking cannabis, was
told by Mr Justice Thesiger:
   "I always doubt whether someone of a public
school education gains much for borstal training. He
may even be a danger, through being regarded by
others as a potential leader of escapes by virtue of
his superior education."'

When the going gets tough, the ex-public school lads

get going. This report in the *Yorkshire Post* once more applauds that character-building experience, plus the secret ingredient:

> 'The legion was a crack force all right, and
> produced very professional, callous killers without
> an ounce of red camaraderie. Its idea of fair play
> was a kick in the crotch, and that Murray preserved
> his sanity says much for a public school education
> and his occasional food parcels from Fortnum
> and Mason.'

These schools do seem to breed a loyalty towards good old Tory values which, in the eyes of some at least, must never be rejected:

> 'It is improbable that any of the few renegade
> public school men who belong to the Socialist
> Party wear the ties of the schools which they have
> dishonoured.'
>
> **(Letter in the *Evening Standard*)**

'Conservative' with a small 'c' does seem to figure prominently in Harrow, where once Mr A.F. Boissier explained on his appointment:

> 'We are a conservative school, and I am a
> conservative man. I see no necessity for any
> important changes. Times may change, conditions
> may change, but the schoolboy remains the same
> for ever. Thus has the zealot of 1919 mellowed with
> the years.'
>
> **(*Sunday Times*)**

Public schools also, it seems, develop their own unique

sense of humour *à la mode* of the 'I say, it's old Squiffy, or Tubs, or Ralgex II . . .' The *Daily Mail* had us waiting with bated breath:

> **'The great moment came when the umpire, W.A.J. West, one of the most famous umpires of all time, could not be found for the group. "Where's West?" we asked. "He's gone west," swiftly retorted Mr Stocks, maintaining the highest traditions of Uppingham humour.'**

The humour associated with public schools is not only that type of sharp intellectual banter, but also the slapstick 'dorm' variety which would appear to continue well into dotage – something which can be gleaned from this request in *The Times*:

> **'Will the numerous Harrovians who, in attempting to divest a very old Etonian of his trousers, deprived him of two treasured five shilling pieces and gold safety-pin, please return one or all to the Army and Navy Club?'**

Detachment from the realities of life emerge humorously from the statements of ex-public school men:

> **'Sir, it was, I think, a chaplain at Winchester School whose opening words to the congregation were: "Few of us can deny the pleasure of speculating on the precise nature of the Pentecostal gift."'**

Well, it certainly wasn't the Curate at St Pat's, Dipton, County Durham!

It does seem a pity that the authorities governing

sartorial elegance at one of our leading public schools
should be such spoil-sports when a touch of initiative
has been demonstrated. The *Daily Telegraph* reported
their plea:

> **'The Committee deplores the fact that unofficial
> Old Rugberian ties are being sold with the stripes
> running the wrong way. These can be sold more
> cheaply because, if the direction of the stripe does
> not matter, it is possible to cut more ties out of
> a given piece of material. Members are urged to
> remain faithful to the official variety.'**

It is the standards which they set through a rigorous
régime which attract so many parents and clearly these
standards are not being eroded, as this snip from the
Evening Standard indicates:

> **'A Hampshire friend reports that an entry in
> her eight-year-old son's diary has convinced her
> that strict discipline continues to be maintained
> in British boarding schools. The entry reads: "I
> must not clean my teeth with salad cream during
> prayers."'**

It is also a discipline and pedigree which makes those who experience it attractive to fellow souls in later life:

> **'A brace of gentlemen needed for Onslow Square flat; must be public school, English, Tory and heterosexual.'**
>
> **(Advert in *The Times*)**

Would it be an advantage to be nicknamed 'Biffy', 'Fatso' or 'Bonzo', one wonders?

The opportunities afforded someone who has had such an education can be huge:

> **'Soon after leaving a boarding school at Harrogate, Mrs ····· entered café society in West Hartlepool.'**
>
> **(*Daily Mail*)**

Hartlepudlians, however, would interpret this as meaning she obtained a job in '*The Yorkshire Lassie*' along York Road, making bacon butties. Sometimes there is disatisfaction expressed on the provision made by even the foremost public schools, according to a Mr Burbank, writing in the *Oxford Mail*:

> **'I often felt his Harrow education did not prepare him for middle eastern intrigue. We discussed sending him to Oxford. In the universities, you get a wider atmosphere.'**

Public school can make a contribution in the most unexpected ways. Who would believe this report from the *Sunday Times*:

> **'Public School boys are being asked to help**

train prospective Labour MPs by acting as
hostile audiences while the Socialists make test
speeches. Colleges and schools on the south coast
are being invited to provide Sixth Form groups
capable of mounting a barrage of heckling at
residential training courses held at Brighton by the
Amalgamated Engineering Union.'

These boys, presumably, will be expressing their Tory
values. If girls had been chosen, then the conflict
would not have been as dramatic, since, as the *Daily
Telegraph* says:

'There is nothing like an English girls' boarding
school for giving a balanced democratic
approach to life.'

Our boarding schools provide, according to one
Observer reporter,

'. . . all those secure places where youths can be
detained for years – suffering no end of short, sharp
shocks – without necessarily having committed any
offence whatsoever.'
   'Mind you,' he continues, 'the results can be a
bit odd. Take, for instance, the curious boyhood
experience of a man I know. He was packed off to a
rather grand public school.'
   'He did not know what he had done to deserve
it, but there he was. Eventually his father rolled
up to take him out for the day – and collected the
wrong boy!'

One is reminded of the occasion when the Earl of
Leicester in the mid-nineteenth century was sitting at

the head of the table at a banquet and enquired of his equerry who the young man was seated half-way down the table:

> 'That, my Lord, is your son!' he replied.

It would also seem, according to a report in the *Observer*, that the public schools hold the answer to the social problems of broken marriages:

> 'The middle classes have reacted to the new freedom – to the emphasis on individual exploration and satisfaction – by getting divorced in large and increasing numbers. From about 1960 on, more and more schools saw they had a rôle providing a stable and secure background for boys and girls from broken homes. It is an example of how subtle and instant is the public schools' response to any basic need in their market.'

In conclusion, one wonders if this advert in *The Times* could be a response to the economic needs of royalty?

> 'Titled boarders accepted *gratis*. Excellent seaside boys' school.'

14
Politicians

Politicians, both nationally and locally, exert a major influence upon education. As the democratically-elected representatives, they are accountable for what goes on in our education establishments, and they can make or break schools. Many are supportive, far-sighted, understanding and considerate – others have done for education what myxomatosis did for rabbits. Recent Tory governments blow their own statistical trumpets to their detriment, as is so succinctly demonstrated by one senior Conservative politician writing in the *Daily Express*:

> '**Mr Hurd made clear yesterday that he could not anticipate the outcome of negotiations, but he emphasized the high rise in police expenditure under the Tory government. Expenditure last year was 50 per cent higher in real terms than in 1978–9. Compare that with 30 per cent for the NHS, 8 per cent for education, 23 per cent for defence.**'

Mr Baker, a member of the Conservative cabinet and

a former Secretary of State for Education, showed on one occasion, according to the *Times Educational Supplement*, an amazing lack of tact:

> 'Additionally, there is little doubt that, outside the core, the curricular guidelines will be far less specific, with the exception, perhaps, of technology, and Mr Baker's pet, history. But one can hardly expect sensitivity from a man who reads *The Charge of the Light Brigade* to a class of Russian children.'

From time to time senior national politicians appear to be completely out of touch, in their dotage or, to be fair to them, inaccurately reported. Surely the latter is the fairest interpretation to put on the comments of Tony Benn, a former Labour Minister and Member of Parliament for over 45 years:

> 'Speaking at Bristol Polytechnic last night . . . he said that there is a great revolution under way in education. "My education policy is to raise the school leaving age to 65."'
>
> *(Evening Post)*

Well, that would certainly solve the employment problem!

At a local level, promoters of educational provision have sometimes to face the ingrained prejudices and deep-rooted beliefs of powerful individuals. Michelangelo, who once said:

> 'If people knew how hard I work to gain my mastery, it would not seem wonderful at all!'

would have thrown down his hammer and chisel at
this observation carried in the *Eastbourne Herald*:

> **'The Mayor then asked if an expenditure of £2,700**
> **a year on an Art School was justified. Culture, he**
> **said, was something that was innate. It could not be**
> **superimposed.'**

Worcester Mayor, Councillor Mrs F.R. Ratcliffe,
may have suffered the backlash of her colleague's
observation from the city's thirsty-for-culture pupils,
because she bitterly complains:

> **'Schoolboys don't raise their caps to me. I was**
> **always taught to look up to my betters. I speak for**
> **all mayors.'**
>
> **(News Chronicle)**

In the West Midlands the *Guardian* reports the comments of a councillor who not only denigrates education, but does so in provocative, sugary language:

> **'The Chairman of the West Midlands Police**
> **Committee yesterday called for the trimming of**
> **"candy floss" items such as education and social**
> **services, so that more money would be available for**
> **the police.'**

Culture, like beauty, is in the eyes of the beholder,
if this report in the *Daily Mirror* is anything to go
by. In Great Yarmouth, there was a popular proposal
to name new roads after Byron, Chaucer, Milton,
Shakespeare and Tennyson. However, Councillor R.F.
Kerrison declared at Yarmouth Town Council:

'"In my opinion, the moral character of these
people is not such that we should name new roads
after them!" He suggested that the roads should be
named after present councillors.'

Now there is a man with his finger on the pulse of
the electorate! Alan Charlton, MP, reported in the
Manchester Evening News, seems likewise to know
what really motivates the common man:

'"Many people," he said, "lived in the slums solely
that their children might be enabled to attend
Church schools."'

The poor middle classes, according to Lt. Col.
Bromley-Davenport, in the *News Chronicle*, were
heading for a fate worse than death:

'"They deserved a break," he said, "before
their backs were broken. They had sold their
homes, spent their savings and were losing their
independence. Some had even been obliged to send
their children to state schools."'

Oh, the shame of it all!
Major Robert Hoare, Master of the Cottesmore
Hunt, reported in the *Sun*, surely represents popular
opinion and the sentiments of the 'Great Unwashed':

'When I was at school and boxed a much bigger
boy who gave me a bloody nose, I didn't lie down
and think "This is awful, I am going to die!" I
thought: "By God, I am going to give him an even

**bloodier nose!" I am sure this is how a fox feels. He
is a braver and better fighter than I will ever be.'**

Very humble of you to denigrate yourself with that last
sentiment, Major, but let's not just take your word for
it. How about sticking some aniseed on your butt-end
and sending you scurrying into the distance before the
hounds are released!

The provision of equality of opportunity seems fine
to some politicians as long as money does not have to
be allocated. The *Yorkshire Post* carried this story of a
meeting in which there was agreement that too much
money was being spent on education. Councillor
Gowen had some points to make:

> '**"At the Institute of Technology," he said,
> "there are sumptuous restaurants instead of
> canteens. No longer do they live in lodgings,
> but in large and modern hostels. It's fantastic!
> In 10 years' time we will be having road
> sweepers with BScs." As he was saying
> "expenditure on education has gone stone
> stark staring mad", a woman from the hall
> shouted, "Yes, and who's going to work
> the mills?"'**

While they're at it, why not bring back transportation!

Finances are, of course, uppermost in the minds
of the majority of politicians, and some will concoct the most bizarre reasons to cut costs. The
Newport Adviser gave this politician the opportunity
to issue a dire warning in this 'green and pleasant land':

'Perverts hiding in bushes and preying on the children of Church Aston could be an unwelcome side effect of tree planting, a parish councillor has warned.'

The *Catholic Times* warned its readers of a different menace:

'The communists were endeavouring to create a state of chaos so necessary for the success of their teaching. They were even infiltrating into knitting and sewing classes.'

Presumably in an effort to stitch everything up!

The 'Red menace' seems to have been discovered in the most innocuous of schemes in the locality of the *Herts and Hemel Hempstead Gazette*:

'A plan to give Hemel Hempstead children an Adventure Playground was condemned as "dangerous and communistic" by a member of the Borough Council's Parks Committee on Tuesday. Declared Councillor Tom Hunter; "By doing this

we shall become communistic in our outlook by encouraging the state control of children."'

It is good that, amid these concerns over our Christian values and heritage, there is a politician who has looked to the positive and clearly believes in the hereafter. The *Hoylake and West Kirby News* printed Councillor Edwards's challenge:

> 'The school is next to a graveyard, so what is wrong with building a funeral parlour? Let's breathe a bit of life into the place!'

Morally it would seem that the 'left' have it over the 'extreme-left' when it comes to modesty, according to this story in the *Evening Standard*:

> 'Some of the students went to sleep, but most of them went swimming. They had managed to open the door to the pool in the basement. The socialists wore their underclothes, and the anarchists didn't.'

At the end of the day, what is needed from a politician is a clear plan which has been formulated by a concise and committed mind from someone who is consistent and unwavering:

> 'Mr Arthur Clark, a 60-year-old independent politician, is to stand in a local by-election on a "Bring Back Grammar Schools, 11-Plus, Anti-Common Market" platform. Interviewed during his campaign, Mr Clark said he was a born-again Christian and a former member of the Labour Party who had belonged to the Conservative Party for five years by mistake.'

Postscript

COMMENTS, OBSERVATIONS AND CONSTRUC-
TIVE CRITICISM . . . on the present Volume would be
welcomed by the compilers, as would any suggestions
or contributions (anecdotes, newspaper cuttings, and
so on) for Volume 2.

Please quote source, data, and any other relevant
information, and send to:

51 Kader Avenue
Acklam
MIDDLESBROUGH
Cleveland
TS5 8NH